BUSHWACK

BUSHWACK

Richard S. Wheeler

CHIVERS

British Library Cataloguing in Publication Data available

This Large Print edition published by AudioGO Ltd, Bath, 2013.
Published by arrangement with Golden West Literary Agency

U.K. Hardcover   ISBN   978 1 4713 4646 0
U.K. Softcover   ISBN   978 1 4713 4647 7

Printed and bound in Great Britain by T J International Limited

BUSHWACK

CHAPTER ONE

She heard one last ragged rasp of breath, and then a silence that stretched taut as the seconds ticked by. The faint movement of his chest stopped and some strange new quality lowered upon his features.

She stood up then, and the morning sun dazzling off the snow blinded her. Randy was dead. She wondered why she wasn't crying. Perhaps it was all too new. Since yesterday, when she knew he was sinking, she had been preparing for this moment. She thought she would break into great broken sobs when it happened.

She looked into the face of her husband, now serene and waxen. Eight months, she thought bitterly. Married June 24, 1882, widowed March 3, 1883.

He had survived the vicious Montana winter with ease. It was she who had huddled around the potbellied stove and the Home Comfort kitchen range, she who had fought off sniffles and fevers through their first cold months in the wilderness. But then with the first flush of warmth, and a hint of thawing in the winds, he had gotten pneumonia while out hunting for cattle and had died four days later.

She was strangely calm, devoid of all feeling. She didn't know what to do; she had no experience of death. She sat on his bed, pulled up the comforter, and folded his hands across his chest.

He looked to be only asleep. The first time she had seen him like that, with the cares of the day absent from his face, was on their honeymoon trip to the Yellowstone country.

It was cold. She threw another chunk of pine into the stove and warmed her hands. There wasn't much wood left. Randy hadn't had time to cut a great deal and was using mostly deadfall from the ponderosa on the slopes. She stepped out to the woodpile and found it was gone. Only one frozen chunk left. She peered out at the bunkhouse. There was no wood piled there, either. She had to have wood. The house would be icy in an hour without it. But somehow it didn't matter much now.

"Why don't I cry?" she kept asking herself. "Don't I love him?" But no tears came, and she stood in the log-walled room in grave solitude. The Reeds all had an unusual amount of self-control, she remembered. It was that quality that made her father, James P. Reed, one of New York's most formidable financiers and a director of the Northern Pacific Railroad. Still, she wondered if something were the matter with her now.

Eight months. The wedding was still vivid in her mind. She saw herself walking toward the altar on the arm of her father, so grave and happy in his morning coat, there at St. Thomas's on Fifth Avenue. And she remembered the look on Randall A. Van Pelt's face when he beheld her there.

It was Randy's distant cousin Theodore Roosevelt who urged them to honeymoon in the Yellowstone country in the Wild West. To camp under the stars, see the amazing geysers, and discover the mountain wilderness.

She brushed a wisp of her honey-red hair back from her face — Randy had started to call her sorrel out here — and stared out upon the blinding snow. She was twenty-two and a widow, she thought. The fierce white light made her green eyes water, and she turned back into the gloom.

She had to get help. She doubted she had the strength to lift Randy from his bed. He had to be buried. She didn't know whether to bury him here in this wilderness or take him East on the train. She recoiled at that, though she knew the Van Pelts would desire it.

But she was alone, snowbound, and over forty miles from Billings where she could board the Northern Pacific. She wasn't even sure she could find her way out of this Bull Mountain wilderness, this tangle of tawny sandstone bluffs, rugged coulees, ponderosa-covered slopes, and grassy parks.

Perhaps she could get to Roundup, she thought. Men would be there at the saloon or the store. She would have to ride seven miles — or did Randy say it was nine? — to the wagon road and north another twenty.

For the first time she questioned the wild impulse that had brought them here. It had started as an adventure, a lark, something to tell all those butterflies in Manhattan about.

She sat down, full of memories, and now at last emotion began to well up from some deep place in her heart. A few hours before her wedding her mother had slipped into her room and sat quietly on the bed.

"Linda dear," she had said, "don't expect too much at first. Honeymoons are often disappointing, and you'll be thinking, Is this all there is?" Linda had known her mother was touching delicately upon things that went unsaid, and she knew her mother was wise. "Give it time, dear. You'll be strangers, even though you think you know and love Randall well. The joys of being a woman will come, but in a year or two . . ."

And that was the way it seemed to Linda at first, the night of her wedding, and then on the Pullman going West. She was happy with Randy, but inside she kept asking, "Is this all?" Then they had arrived at Yellowstone, and things changed.

Was it the mountain air? The rushing, cold falls? The campfire smell? The huge appetites they suddenly acquired? The fleeting moon and necklaces of stars? She couldn't say. She knew only that she and Randy had come alive in the wilderness, and some primal stirring in their hearts and bodies had transported them. After a month spent camping, and sometimes in log lodges, New York had lost all its glitter.

Linda sighed. The memories filled her with painful tenderness. She looked at the waxen face in the bedroom and felt the beginnings of agony and fear.

They had started talking about staying in the West, at least for a year or two. Randy wanted a ranch. He knew nothing about ranching, but he never doubted, with his connections, that he could buy the right information and advice. Linda was game for anything, and the more Randy talked of ranching, the more she was enchanted by the adventure.

They had rented a hotel room in Billings, and that was the only time in their marriage that Linda was not altogether happy. The board-and-batt buildings in that crude railroad town were ugly, and she felt hemmed in by the yellow rimrock of the Yellowstone River valley.

Randy had written his parents and hers about the ranch, and James Reed responded by wiring Thomas Bell, the NP's Montana supervisor.

Bell ushered the newlyweds into his office in the Billings station and had gently dissuaded them from a Rocky Mountain ranch, where it was cold and ranching was impractical. "But there's a place north of Billings, up in the Bulls, that would be fine cattle country," he explained. "The Bull Mountains have no flowing water, but there are good springs, earth tanks, and windmill wells for your stock.

"This place I'm thinking of is part homestead, part federal land, and part NP land. The railroad's got every other section through there. Checkerboard pattern. It'd be no problem to trade with the Interior Department and deed forty sections solid to you."

"Does it have a gracious house?" Linda asked.

The supervisor smiled.

"Mrs. Van Pelt, there's hardly a house in Montana you could call gracious by New York standards. The place has a solid log house with three rooms and big sandstone fireplaces. Woodstove heat, outdoor privy, spring water piped in, solid pole corrals, and a large log barn. Solid, rustic, but not *gracious*. Not by a country mile!"

She had blushed.

For two weeks the telegraphs had chattered, and then Randy had his deed, free and clear, and the money to purchase his stock and supplies.

During the next weeks the Van Pelt fortune continued to smooth Randy's path. Expert cattle buyers purchased his herd in Nebraska and instructed him in animal husbandry. Skilled cowboys pushed the herd north from Billings railroad pens and scattered the Herefords through lush valleys. NP freight wagons hauled salt and hay and furniture and groceries north. Knowledgeable railroad buyers gathered a remuda of fine cutting horses, geldings, mares, and a stallion.

By October the newlyweds were settled and alone in their Eden. Linda unpacked her Tiffany silver and Wedgwood china and set an incongruous table in the rustic kitchen before a huge sandstone hearth. Randy rode his ranges and checked his waters until the snow came, and then belatedly began to gather and cut firewood, barely staying ahead. Time whirled by; they were too much in love to notice their isolation.

And then Randy died.

Linda shuddered. She stared bleakly across to the man she had known so intimately, and who had known her the same way, so briefly.

The stove needed tending. The numbing cold that had been poised outside those log walls all winter now seemed to be creeping through, triumphantly driving back the heat until the only warmth left was just around the potbellied heater. She lifted the last log and dropped it on the red coals. It was wet and took a long time to flare. She suddenly realized the cold would kill her, too, unless she got wood immediately — wood for the stove, wood for the kitchen range, wood for the fireplaces. Wood to heat the food she would eat.

She bundled into her new sheepskin and muff, and Randy's leather gloves and india rubber galoshes, and trudged out to the wooded slope behind the ranch buildings. The sun was warmer than she had supposed, but the breezes were bitter. She realized that Randy had stripped the whole slope of its deadwood; indeed, she saw none at all within sight of the ranch.

She trudged north. The snow was mushy on the south slopes but hard on the shadowed ones. At last she spotted a dead limb and swung her ax at it. She barely chipped the bark. Alarmed, she flailed at the ponderosa branch and chipped it. She tried the bucksaw, and at last made some progress when the big teeth bit the pine. Her arms ached by the time the limb cracked down, but she dragged it slowly back to the log house, pausing every few yards to change hands.

Randy had built a sawhorse, and once she dropped the limb onto it, the sawing went easier. She struggled for two hours until she had no more strength, but at last she had kindling and cordwood enough for one night. Just one night.

She was frightened. The ashes in the potbellied stove had died. She decided to forget the stove and light the kitchen range instead, so that one fire would keep her warm and allow her to cook.

She knew ruefully that she was terribly unprepared for this Montana wilderness and that she could easily die. Numbly she shoved kindling and twigs into the stove and scratched a big phosphorous match. The fire took forever to catch, but at last some faint heat radiated from the cook top.

The horses needed to be fed, she remembered. She set some water to boil — she desperately wanted hot tea — and ran out to the corrals. Randy had kept three in and let the others forage. She pitched hay to the big geldings and gave each a couple of quarts of oats. They had nickered to her as she approached, and their friendliness had warmed her. They were the only living things in sight, and suddenly she loved them.

It came to her slowly that they could take her to safety. Wasn't there a neighbor? Randy had met him once. Some bachelor man on the far side of the Roundup road? Someone not very friendly?

The man's name was Parker. Some funny first name that had amused Randy. He raised and trained horses all alone, Randy had said. He was at least ten miles away, if she could find him. On the other side of the road, but which way? South toward Billings?

She racked her mind trying to remember the words she had so casually ignored. Information that could save her life now.

The tea water was bubbling, and a niggardly heat suffused the kitchen when she stepped in. The sight of Randy, still and white in the bedroom, subdued her and unexpectedly the first tears came.

"Oh, Randy, oh Randy," she whispered.

She brewed the tea strong and bitter, and swallowed cup after cup until her strength returned and warmth reached her cold toes. She didn't feel like eating, but she forced herself to swallow some broth against the hard afternoon she faced.

A wave of homesickness ran through her. The thought of her father, with his piercing eyes and resolute will somehow comforted her. They always said in the Reed family that she had inherited her father's iron will along with his red hair.

Encouraged by the memory, she steeled herself. Linda Van Pelt swept swiftly through her home, gathering the things upon which her life would depend. Into a burlap bag she put food for three days, cooking gear, matches, knives. Into a second bag she stuffed blankets, gloves, extra boots, emergency kindling. She found a half-empty bag of oats in the barn and decided to take that too.

If she hurried, she could find the neighbor before dusk. If not — she'd survive if she were careful. She saddled Liberty, the big bay, and then cinched Randy's saddle on Marty, the lineback dun. Then she turned out Mother-in-Law to fend for herself.

She pulled the door of the house tight and checked it to make sure no animals could slip in. Then she leaped easily to the saddle and felt its coldness force its way up to her body.

She turned to gaze at this good and solid ranch, desolate in the bright, warm sun. Any other time, she would have thought it was handsome. The log home radiated comfort and security. The solid pole corrals and well-tended yards spoke of things well built and well cared for.

Golden grass poked through the patched snow, and the black log buildings nestled beneath tawny sandstone bluffs. It all stirred her heart. This land, so wild and beautiful, had its grip upon her still, even though it had stolen the life of her husband.

The trail to the wagon road was covered with patches of snow, but she knew it well enough. She led Marty with a halter rope but found she didn't need it, and released him to follow as he would.

By the time she was a quarter of a mile on her way, she knew she had trouble. Iceballs had built up under the hooves of both geldings, and they could scarcely hobble. She rummaged for a knife and cut away the hardened slush from all eight hooves. At that rate it would take forever to reach safety, she thought grimly.

She was not a woman who let difficulties flatten her. She veered for bare spots and tried several gaits to see if one would shake the iceballs loose. She loped once but stopped suddenly when the gelding skidded.

Nothing worked well, and she was forced to dismount over and over. Time raced and the winter shadows lengthened while she was still far from the road.

As fast as the sun lowered, the relentless cold bore in, through her sheepskin, through Randy's woolly chaps. Frost collected along the withers and flanks of the horses.

She jumped off Liberty and led him for a while to get her own blood moving. The country had become confusing in the dusk: the shadowed hills looked so alike, and the valley she followed sometimes branched in several directions.

Linda knew the wind had hollowed countless shallow caves in the sandstone outcrops, and if worse came to worse, she would hunt one. That would be a last resort, she decided, as she plunged westward with determination.

She remembered suddenly she hadn't brought Randy's pistol. She was unarmed against wolves, bears, coyotes — or men. The thought added to her somber burden and she resisted the impulse to weep.

The night lowered harshly and the cold hardened the slush. She realized she was covering more ground between hoof-cleaning stops. She found the Big Dipper and the North Star and kept it firmly at her right because she was lost now and had no idea how far she had strayed from her trail. She knew only that if she headed west, she would find the road.

There was no moon, but the snow reflected the starlight dully and she could see ahead.

"This wilderness is no place for cowards," she said aloud to Liberty. She began to feel more secure. Some commanding presence had risen within her, a reflection of her father's will. She was surviving! She was alive and decently warm in an empty, icy wilderness.

She almost missed the road because she struck it at a rocky barren place where the tracks were few. But a backward glance had directed her to some ruts to the right. She halted and rubbed her glove down Liberty's neck.

Roundup was perhaps twenty miles north, but there was only a saloon, a store, and a rude stage stop, and it was a hangout for rough characters. Billings was south nearly forty miles, across windswept rolling prairie. But the railroad was there. And help. And the telegraph. And a warm, safe hotel room.

She turned south.

Scarcely ten minutes later she saw an orange light flickering dully west of the road. The neighbor! A vast, warm flood of joy swept through her. She found the turnoff and urged the bay and the dun up a grade, then into a coulee, and finally onto a small meadow nestled under hills on three sides.

The cabin, with fragrant wood smoke lowering from the chimney, was the smallest she could imagine, with mud-chinked logs and a wood shake roof. A larger log barn with a sod roof stood at her left. High pole corrals surrounded the barn, and she could see several horses peering at her. One of them whinnied.

Liberty whinnied back, and then the door

opened and a tall man was silhouetted in the lamplight.

CHAPTER TWO

He thought better of targeting himself in the lamplight, so he turned down the wick and reached for the shotgun.

"You out there, put your hands up," he called softly into the icy night.

"Sir . . . I need help," Linda replied.

"You didn't hail the house," he barked. "Get down slowly and walk toward me."

She did, while the gelding breathed clouds of vapor into the night. "I'm new in the West. I'm sorry," she said.

He paused, surprised to discover a bundled-up woman emerging from the gloom.

"Could have got yourself shot," he grumbled. "You intending to stay? If so, I'd better get your horses in."

"I — yes. No, not stay. I mean —"

"Tell me in a minute," he said as he plunged past her. He gathered the two geldings, pushed them into an empty pen, stripped off the gear, and forked them some native-grass hay.

She felt a wave of relaxing warmth on her cheeks as she entered. She turned up the lamp and discovered she was in an incredibly small log cabin, perhaps twelve by fifteen feet.

There was a brass bed in one corner, a dresser and washstand, a kitchen range and cabinet, and a chair. That was all. A tiny fortress against the Montana winter, she thought.

"I fed them your oats," he said as he came in. He stared at the girl as she pulled off her cap and released a cascade of red hair. "Who are you?"

"Linda Van Pelt."

"Van Pelt? I met your husband last fall. Out riding. Or was it your husband?"

"Yes it was," she replied. "And your last name is Parker?"

"Canada Parker. I'll tell you before you ask. I was born on the coldest day of winter and that's the name they hung on me."

"I wasn't going to ask," she replied stiffly. "I need help. My husband died this morning."

A silence flowed across the little room and she stared at him. She realized he was very tall and almost skeleton thin, with cold gray

24

eyes. There was a quality about him, she realized, an aura, a sadness and gentleness. She was suddenly reminded of a portrait of Abe Lincoln that had touched her once.

"I'm sorry to hear it," he said slowly. "How'd it happen?"

"Pneumonia, I think. He got a fever and his lungs were congested and then he just faded away . . ."

"Well, what can I do for you?" He meant it kindly, but it sounded abrupt to her. Everything he said had been abrupt. She stared at him uncertainly, then at the whitewashed log walls and the rough-sawn plank floor, swept immaculately clean.

"I don't know," she said. "I think I'd better go on to Billings."

"You're thinking you don't dare trust a strange man. You're thinking you're a lone woman and vulnerable," he said severely. "I don't like that."

She flushed.

He smiled suddenly. "Look," he said softly. "No honorable man would — treat you badly — in your circumstances. And you're in the West. There's some unwritten rules about women out here."

She relaxed in the new warmth.

"Now please accept my hospitality and let's figure what to do," he said. "I'll help you out of those duds."

Wordlessly she pulled off the woolly chaps and heavy sheepskin, and as he surveyed her, he realized that beneath the bulky man's shirt and dungarees was the thin, angular figure of a pretty young woman. She moved to the stove and warmed her hands over it.

"I'd like to help," he said, breaking the silence.

"There's no wood. He didn't leave any. I tried to get some," she said abruptly. "He's, he's — lying there in the bed."

He waited for her to continue, wondering what sort of young fools would plunge into a Montana winter without plentiful cordwood.

She held her hands over the stove as she talked.

"When he died, I didn't know what to do. I don't have a coffin or anything. I don't know whether to bury him here or in New York. I just . . . I have to wire his family, too. And mine. I — I can't even lift him from the bed. I can't just *leave* him there . . ."

She stared at him and a wave of desolation rolled through her. Tears quickened upon her cheeks. Now, in the presence of another human being, the grief she had held

26

back all day rose up within her and flooded her.

He wished he could hold her. She needed to be held tight by someone who could share her grief.

"We were married last June," she said through tears. "It's so wrong, so cruel."

"I can't comfort you much. A body needs to grieve," he said quietly. "A person should have old friends or folks at hand, and I'm neither."

"I'm sorry to trouble you," she whispered.

"No trouble at all, Mrs. Van Pelt" — he wanted to call her Linda — "and I'm just glad you got here safely. I can take care of everything. No trouble at all."

She turned away from the stove and sat down wearily, utterly exhausted by the cruel day.

"Look," he said uncomfortably. "You'd better get some sleep, and tomorrow we'll ride back and I'll take care of everything. I've got some canvas for a shroud, and we'll take Mr. Van Pelt — him — to Billings in my buckboard. And cut you some firewood if you plan to stay. And get you a hotel if you don't."

She stared up into his gray eyes and then involuntarily toward the brass bed, and then the tears came again.

Canada Parker saw the tears and misunderstood.

"I'm going to sleep in the barn," he said edgily, "just as fast as I can round up some blankets and a few woollies."

She was too immersed in memories of Randy to think much about it.

"There's plenty of wood there, but even with the stove dampened down, you'll have to stoke up the fire in the night — unless you want ice in the washbowl in the morning. Tomorrow we'll have breakfast and coffee an' — say, are you hungry? Have you eaten?"

Linda emerged from her private sorrowing and smiled wanly at Canada.

"No I haven't, but I'm not hungry," she replied.

"Maybe you ain't, but you're going to have some tea," he said sternly. He opened a canister, poured some hot water from the ever-ready teakettle on the stove, and shoved the cup into her hands. She sipped it black, and liked the strong masculine taste on her tongue.

He watched the thin woman sip the steaming tea for a moment, sighed, and gathered up a pile of blankets.

"Thunder mug under the bed," he

mumbled, embarrassed. "Or left, outside. Night."

The door banged behind him, and he trudged through the icy air to the barn, feeling sorry for himself. It was a little warmer in the blackness, under the sod roof. He burrowed into a high mound of hay until he made a small cavern, and then rolled himself up in two blankets and pulled the hay down over him. The warmth came slowly and he shivered unrelentingly.

A few minutes later he heard her outside the barn.

"Canada" — she used his first name — "Canada, I've been perfectly thoughtless. You'll freeze there. Please — I'll sleep on the floor beside the stove . . ."

He heard a sweetness in her voice that had been absent before. And it was an invitation he had no second thoughts about accepting.

"It's a mite cool at that," he allowed as he stretched up in the blackness. "If it's no account to you, I'll come in."

They walked to the cabin together under stars like crystals of ice. He shook the hay out of his blankets and unrolled them beside the kitchen range.

"I'll stay here," he said firmly, and she didn't argue. She unlaced her boots and then rolled beneath the comforter on the brass bed.

"Canada," she whispered softly, "thank you from the bottom of my heart."

She was soon deep in exhausted sleep, but he lay awake on the hard floor, in low spirits, aware of the slender freckled red-head, the New York City bride, who unconsciously radiated the grace and good manners of her people. He was troubled by a nameless yearning that melded into pain. He had known too much loneliness and failure; too many things had gone wrong. He drifted into fitful sleep.

Linda was awakened by the mingled aromas of coffee and bacon and the sound of fire crackling in the stove. The man wasn't Randy; he was much taller and a little thinner. She stared at him from beneath her comforter, and recollected things that had brought her here and had caused her to spend a night in this tiny cabin with the stranger. She knew it was not something she could readily explain to her parents or friends or anyone back East.

She realized she knew nothing about him, so she watched as he busied himself. There were circles under his eyes, and she felt guilty. He seemed just a little stooped, as if carrying an invisible heavy burden upon his shoulders, and the sadness she had noticed the night before seemed all the more upon him today.

"Good morning," he said solemnly, fixing her with his gray direct eyes. She felt the intimacy of the situation, this stranger staring at her in bed, and she whirled the comforter off suddenly, sat up, and smoothed her rumpled shirt and dungarees.

He moved the frying pan to a cool corner of the range and disappeared outside in a burst of sunshine. She watched him in the corrals, pitching hay to several horses, rubbing their jaws and scratching their ears with an old, established camaraderie. He slipped a halter over one fine sorrel mare and led her to another pen and gave her a bucket of oats. Linda noticed that the sadness seemed to lift from him out there among his horses. He laughed at one and patted another and slapped a sorrel playfully across the rump. And even through the glass she heard nickering and whinnying and happy uproar. She was fascinated: Canada Parker was transformed out in the winter sun with his furry horses.

She realized he had left her alone purposefully, and she poured icy water into a washbasin and added some hot from the teakettle, and scrubbed her face. There was a brush, and she examined it hesitantly, and then pulled it happily through her tangled sorrel knots until her scalp tingled and she saw herself glossy in the early sun. She opened the front door and threw out the wash water, and he took it as the signal to come in.

The sadness lowered upon him again as he entered, and it was a palpable presence that Linda felt. She wanted to cheer him, even though it was she who grieved this morning.

"How much snow was there coming here?" he asked.

"Sometimes it reached Liberty's knees," she replied.

He frowned. "I'll have to try to get through with the buckboard," he said. "I'll take a shovel."

"You're a good cook," she said, eating ravenously as she sat on the edge of the bed.

"Lots of experience at it," he said dourly.

She understood the hidden meaning.

"I'm going to turn out my horses," he said. "They can feed pretty well on the south slopes, now that the sun has opened up the snow a little. Then I can stay over there as long as you need help."

"I'm sorry, I didn't mean to inconvenience

you," she said. "Do you have many horses here?"

"Yup. I train them to saddle and harness. You'd be surprised how many outfits want finished horses instead of range broncs. Need 'em for buggies, and wives, and old men. Cowboys want 'em too, though they're always bragging about riding the hurricane decks. But lots of 'em get smashed up doing that and then they lay out a month's pay for one of mine. So it's mostly horses, except for a dozen cows I keep around for beef or a quick sale."

"Is this a big place?" she asked. She was enjoying the way he opened up to her when they got onto the topic of horses.

"No. Three-hundred-twenty-acre homestead. I lease three and a half sections from the NP railroad and three more from the Interior Department. Built all this myself, though I'm no carpenter, that's for sure."

She carried her empty plate to the washstand. "I'll do your dishes," she said. "That'll save time."

She watched him as she scrubbed. He slipped the collar and hames over the big red mare, and then the bellyband, traces, and reins. Then he fetched another big mare that Linda hadn't noticed, and harnessed her. He backed the pair up to the whiffletree and hooked up. Then he loaded in Linda's food, some blankets, his own saddle, and a roll of canvas.

By the time she had bundled herself in Randy's chaps and sheepskin, Canada had added her saddle, a shovel, and a pickax to the pile in the buckboard. Then he shooed the horses out of the corrals, lifted Linda to her seat, tied her geldings behind, and climbed aboard.

He paused, sniffing the wind. "It's a chinook," he said. "Feel that breeze? It'll strip off the snow in hours and the temperature will likely hit sixty this afternoon."

"I've heard of chinooks," she said. "Isn't that what we had a month ago?"

"That was it," he said. "Warm air off the Pacific, they tell me. Blows the cold right out. . . . We'd better hurry."

"Hurry?"

He looked at her. "In a few hours we could be up to our axles in mud," he said, thinking of certain difficulties that would affect Linda's plans.

He wheeled the mares north, up the sloppy wagon road, past outcrops of sandstone sandwiched with layers of coal.

"Does your place have coal exposed like that?" he asked.

"Yes. Randy showed me several spots."

"Good. That'll give us some quick fuel."

An uncanny warmth permeated the air and the sun pummeled fragrance from the ponderosa. Canada turned the mares east into flat, wet snow at a place where Linda couldn't imagine a road, and she turned to watch the furrows stretch out behind the buckboard's iron tires.

They rode in silence for an hour, drinking in the glorious warmth as they clattered through grassy parks lying between dark, pine-dotted slopes. She tried to think of Randy, almost as if some duty required it, and she was disturbed because she couldn't remember the timbre of his voice, nor could she recollect his little gestures. She tried hard to think of them, and slipped into a new melancholy.

"Thinking about him?" Canada asked. "It's right to grieve. Never bottle it up."

The going was heavier as the sun climbed, but there was still a hard-frozen surface underneath the slush.

"Should I ride Liberty? That would lighten the buckboard," she asked suddenly.

"Nope, not yet," he said. "Linda — may I call you that? — do you realize this could turn the roads into quagmires for many days?"

"Yes."

"Do you know what I'm driving at?"

"Yes," she whispered.

He changed the subject. "We're on your land now, I believe. Should be seeing some of your Herefords. You've got the only pure-blood herd in this country. . . . How many did you move up here last fall?"

"Eight hundred. My father bought them for us. Or he had a man do it, and they came on a train from Nebraska. There were something like three hundred bred heifers, and the rest were mostly cows and a few bulls. Almost no steers."

"You know a lot for a New York girl," Canada mused. "We should be seeing some soon. What's the brand?"

"VP — Van Pelt, on the left thigh," she said. "The older cows and bulls also have a T-Bar."

"Did Randy notice any winterkill?"

"Yes — it's funny you asked that. He was having trouble finding them all, and riding everywhere looking for them. And . . . that's how he got pneumonia."

"Forty sections is a lot of land," Canada said. "They're probably bunched up in some far valley. With this up-and-down country, with all these coulees, you can hide a passel of 'em in a hurry."

"I suppose so," she said. "But the last

36

thing he talked about was the missing cattle."

"I'm hunting a dozen horses myself," Canada said. "Darned things got wild on me through the winter. I've been out all week scrounging for them, but they're hunkered down in one of those locked-up valleys off yonder to the west. It keeps troubling me, though. Two of them were good-looking blooded stallions, and some others were quarter and Morgan mares."

"There's my tracks from last night," she said. "I got off the road."

"Easy to do at night. There's not a prominent landmark in all the Bulls. Just hill and coulee country, except maybe that blue mesa off southeast. I imagine we'll be cutting the tracks of those old cows pretty soon, and then we can get a line on them. They don't kill easily, especially here where they've got all the shelter they need in the pines and sandstone. Maybe I'll be able to track 'em down for you."

They topped a low divide between sandstone pillars and followed the road north along a descending grade. The wagon slid and pressed forward against the mares.

"Won't be long now before it's all mud," he said.

They pulled off their caps and unbuttoned

their coats in the fragrant air and rode silently with nothing but the clopping hooves and creaking buckboard to disturb their reveries. Each was secretly grateful for the company.

"You know more about me than I know about you," she said.

"What would you like to know?" he asked with a certain reserve.

"Only what you'd like me to."

He grinned. She knew more about the ways of the West than she let on, he decided.

"Canada Parker's the world's number one flop," he began wryly. "My folks in Dakota were both dead time I was fourteen. The dryland farm failed, too. I ran a store for a while, but the customers didn't like my sharp tongue. I was a Northern Pacific stationmaster, but they said I was rude to customers and they booted me out. I cowboyed awhile but I was always riling the foreman or owner with my notions. Usually didn't like the way they spoiled horses. So four or five outfits paid up and kicked me off, and another three kicked me off without payin'. Now I'm homesteading and training horses right."

"Sometimes the best men are the ones who have the most difficulty," she said kindly. "People don't like to be shown they're wrong."

"Now you're excusin' me," he snorted. "I was no darn good as a stationmaster, for sure, or keepin' store."

"But you're good with horses."

"Yes, I am that," he agreed.

She liked his quiet response. He was whipcord tough, she realized. More handsome by day than in the lamplight. Appealing in his rough way, especially when he grinned.

"I'm right on the brink of something big," he confided. "Something that'll pay off handsome, high and wide."

She waited, somehow pleased.

"Remounts. Cavalry man from up at Fort McGinnis says they'll buy everything I can raise, long as it's got teeth and four sound legs. They like my stuff."

"Canada — that's grand!"

"It could make me fat in a few years. Heaven knows, I'm sick of bein' poor. Those soldierboys, now, they've got strong notions of what makes a cavalry pony, and those notions just happen to agree with me."

"Such as — ?"

"Good lungs and girth. Solid color. That shows the blood. They don't want any Indian ponies or mustangs. No speed in 'em."

"And you've got the right bloodstock."

"Sure do. I'm the only one in Montana. All solid color. I sold the first up there the other day. Them officers, they're crawlin' over themselves to get one of my trained critters, so I'm asking a good price."

She saw some rare cheerfulness blossom in him.

"Wisht I had a hundred more mares," he grinned.

"You'll get them, Canada, if you reinvest."

"Yup, I will. It'll take some doin' though. I'll have to ship 'em from back East."

"You're like my father. He sees a need and sets out to fill it," she said. "If it's a big need, he isn't afraid to finance a large business."

"I never dreamed big until now," he sighed. "But this here frontier — it makes a man reach!"

"Next thing you know, you'll have a big house on a big ranch." She smiled.

"Big houses ain't what I live for," he said softly.

"Horses are what you live for!" she shot back at him.

He grinned.

By the time they drove into the ranch yard, Canada knew they'd never make it to Billings in the buckboard. With horses, perhaps, but not with a vehicle. For the previous hour, the wagon had furrowed mud and the mares had strained in their harnesses. They were exhausted after ten miles: forty was out of the question.

The ranch house was somber in the sun. He liked the way it nestled against a slope, and the solidity of the bunkhouse, corrals, and barn.

He eyed her, sitting hesitantly in the buckboard, reluctant to step down.

"You have some decisions to make," he said. "Do you want to see him?"

She stared at the log house with the faintly sinister gloominess about it and then took a deep breath that signaled an inner decision.

"No . . . no. I want to remember as he was. The way we were at Yellowstone . . ."

Her eyes met his for a moment.

"You realize we can't make it back to Billings in the buckboard," he said.

"I know. I was watching the mares struggle this last hour in the mud."

"And we can't wait long . . ."

"I know."

"Linda, unhitch the team and put your horses in the pens and stay out here under the good sun, and maybe it'd help if you prayed if you're of a mind to."

He dropped off the seat and turned back

to look at her, sitting mutely, her sorrel hair glistening while the chinook winds played with locks of it. He pulled some cord and the canvas tarp from the wagon and carried them inside. A little later he came out and found her still sitting and the horses restless.

Wordlessly he unhitched the mares and stripped off the harness and led them and her geldings to the pens. He felt her green eyes upon him, questioning, and when he turned, he saw a wetness in them and felt her palpable loneliness.

"Linda," he said gruffly, "I want you to pick a spot. It has to be done."

He lifted a hand, and she took it and stepped down into the slush. She took a deep breath and walked slowly north, up a slope to a low plateau where an arc of ponderosas formed an intimate glade. She looked around, as if remembering something sweet that had happened here, and turned to him.

"Here," she said, and Canada knew that this place held remembrances for her.

He dug the mud away and hit frozen ground a few inches down while she watched silently.

"Where's that coal outcrop?" he asked.

She pointed to one just a hundred yards

distant in a sandstone escarpment. He found a wheelbarrow and his pickax and dug there and then built a coal fire over the burial place.

"That'll take all night," he said.

They walked back to the log house and he saw her hesitation.

"Wait here," he said, and slipped inside. He returned a moment later with a canvas-shrouded burden and carried it to the barn. Then they entered the icy house together, and she noticed that Canada had pulled up the coverlet of Randy's bed and fluffed the pillow and had tried to make death vanish. She felt grateful.

He built large fires in the fireplaces, the stove, and the kitchen range, using all the wood she had cut.

"I have to cut some more and bring some coal," he said, leaving her in her honeymoon home.

He worked through the warm afternoon and by dusk there was a solid pile of sawed logs and chunks of coal outside the kitchen door.

He found her still in the rocking chair where he had left her. He rebuilt the fires and lit the lamps.

"I'm sorry I haven't started a meal," she sighed.

"I didn't expect you to," he replied. "If you want to eat, I can make tolerable flapjacks."

She decided she didn't, but she changed her mind when the aromas rose from Canada's sizzling frying pan.

"My father and I buried my mother in Dakota, and then I buried my father," Canada said while they ate. "I was fourteen and did it alone. No one to help me. I wish there had been someone to read some psalm or say a prayer over him. I just buried him, shoveled back the dirt, and walked away and cried. I was one lonely kid."

"Would you? Tomorrow?" she asked.

"I'll try. Linda, with this chinook around, we may not get to Billings for several days, or even weeks."

"Canada — it's funny, but I'm not in a hurry any more. At first, all I could think of was going East. But what's there? I'll go; I have to. And wire them. But there's nothing there and nothing here."

He carried the dishes to the drainboard and then paused in the warm room.

"I'll go on down to the bunkhouse," he said.

"Canada, that's not necessary! Please stay here in the living room. I don't want to be alone tonight. I need someone here. It'd be

44

very comforting . . ." Her green eyes were directly upon him.

"I'll bunk here, then," he grinned. "I'll get a straw tick from down there and unroll the blankets here. If that suits you.

"And I plan to stay around several days and get things in order for you. Maybe ride around a bit and check on those cattle. I didn't see a single cow track coming in and I'm getting curious about them.

"Sleep well, Linda, sleep well."

CHAPTER THREE

She was expecting him to say something, but he didn't know what to say.

She shivered a little in her summer cotton. The navy blue was the closest thing she had to black. Whenever the sun vanished behind racing clouds, she pulled her shawl tighter.

"I don't know any prayers or anything like that," Canada said.

He knew she wanted some words and now her grave look was a request.

"I only met Randall Van Pelt once," he began, clearing his throat. "It was a neighborly visit. I liked the man, and it felt good having a neighbor only ten miles away . . ."

Canada looked at her and saw that her taut expression had eased a bit.

"When a man's lived long and has achieved a lot, we can point to all his works. He did this and that and the other. But when a man's cut off young, all fresh and starting out in life, what can we say?"

She was listening intently and not staring into the grave any more.

"Mighty few things. He started up a ranch. Got him some education. Was a good son who honored his parents. Took him a wife . . ."

Canada suddenly understood what he needed to say, and his groping for words vanished.

"What he left behind was a treasury of memories," he continued. "Even if the marriage was brief, it was full of memories. Things a bride and groom share. Laughter! Meals together! Sunlight in the mornin'! Dreams and plans! Trip to Yellowstone and the open West!

"So Randall Van Pelt left a treasure of memories with his bride, and changed her with his love. He enriched her, even as she enriched him. She didn't have very many hours with him, but they were all rich. He loved her, and she loved him, and that's what changed her and lifted her up.

"Yes, a mighty fine young man, gracious, with good character . . ."

He ran out of words suddenly and saw she was crying.

"Lord God, we commend the soul of Randall Van Pelt to you now," he concluded.

Then he shoveled while she stood with a

wet face and watched until the cold mud was mounded over the man she had held in her arms.

They walked silently back to the house and warmed themselves.

"Couldn't think of much to say," he apologized.

"Oh, Canada, it was beautiful. Thank you for doing something that was hard to do," she breathed.

He sighed. "I guess I'll go cut wood; we may be here a few days. You just be quiet today, and I'll fix a supper when I get back."

"No, Canada," she said firmly. "I'm coming with you. Sitting here full of misery won't help me a bit. Let me change and I'll come cut wood with you — if you'll have me."

He liked her pluck, and smiled. While she changed he harnessed the mares and hooked them to a sledge he found behind the barn. Then she appeared in her dungarees and woolen shirt, with a cap barely disciplining her red hair.

They worked quietly through the afternoon, saying little but enjoying each other's company. She held one end of the crosscut saw and felt his strength at the other. He lifted the deadwood limbs to the sledge and felt her easing his burden. He saw her cheeks redden with steady work under the chinook sun, and saw the labor put life into her eyes. She saw the sadness lift from him as they cut wood together, but she avoided the thought that her presence might be the reason for the light in his face.

When the shadows were long and lavender in the wet snow, they headed home, she atop the pile of logs while he led the mares.

"My feet are frozen," she laughed. "That sloppy snow got through my boots!"

He unloaded the day's booty, and before he had finished, he smelled the fragrance of her kitchen. When he stomped the mud off his boots and entered the kitchen door, he was amazed. Her table had been set with Wedgwood, crystal-glass goblets, Tiffany silver glinting in the firelight, and candles.

"I don't have much of any way to thank you," she smiled. "And it's better for me to be doing things."

It was true enough, and yet it puzzled him.

They devoured the rib roast and corn bread and creamed onions with appetites that had become ravenous after an afternoon's hard labor. Canada said little, acutely conscious of his rough-hewn manners, scarcely knowing the feel of a linen napkin, aware of the station of the fine woman across from him, ashamed at the thoughts that crowded into his mind on the very day they had buried her husband.

"I'm dead tired," she said suddenly. "It's been a hard day for me, the hardest I've ever had. Please excuse me now."

The door to her bedroom clicked shut, and Canada felt the palpable loneliness of the living room and kitchen. His desolation lowered down upon him again. He scraped and rinsed the dishes moodily, stared darkly into the snapping fire, and finally lowered himself into his makeshift bed. He didn't sleep. He was haunted by the presence, just beyond that door, of the most enchanting woman he had ever known. It wasn't lust that stirred him, but rather the beginning of an impossible love. Guiltily he remembered Randall Van Pelt III.

Sometime — he imagined it was around two — he arose and paced. There was a half-moon casting a pale, cold light across the snow. He dressed then, urgently needing the outdoors and the horses that solaced him with their warmth.

He scribbled a note for her, which said simply that he was riding early, looking for Van Pelt cattle. Then he slipped out into the cold. As fast as the icy night enveloped him, his hungers vanished and he was restored to the real, hard, frontier world where he had been born.

He found his mare and she nickered affectionately. He stroked her muzzle and ran his hand down her neck beneath the mane, loving the good smell of her. His desolation vanished as it always did when he was working with his animals.

Canada threw the saddle blanket over her and then the big roping saddle and drew the latigo tight. He warmed the bit in his hand before slipping it into her mouth. Then he sprang upon her with the effortless grace of a man born to train horses.

The North Star was there to navigate with, and he drifted easterly through the pale light, all alive and as close to peace as his orphaned heart could be. His sheepskin and woolly chaps made the riding pleasant. He was alone with his mare, enjoying her rhythm as it was transmitted through his own body.

It was country to get lost in. The valleys ran in any direction, and some valleys split into a half a dozen arms. He topped ridges, rode beneath bluffs, circled chimney rock and pillars etched by the winds. He saw no cattle.

After three hours of eastward travel he paused as he crested a ridge. The mare's ears had perked up and rotated south, and he expected to see perhaps a deer or even an early bear.

Instead, he heard voices.

He peered hard into the gloom and saw the bulks of four riders moving a dozen or so cows slowly up the valley. Canada reached down to his waist to check his pistol and realized with a jolt that he was unarmed.

He stood stock still then and soothed the mare. There was rank danger now: the slightest suspicion that they had been seen would send those riders after him and they would gun him down as surely as the sun would rise.

Their horses stared at Canada, and he feared he would be discovered. He reached forward and rubbed his mare's ears and neck soothingly.

The black bulk of a cow broke from the bunch, and one of the night riders expertly spurred his horse wide and drove the animal back into the bunch.

"Git in there, you five-hundred-dollar rascal," he yelled loud enough for Canada to hear, and the others chuckled. The wide-looping brethren gradually disappeared into the gloom even as the first dawn light broke grayly ahead.

Canada realized that he was not likely to

find many Van Pelt cattle around, not with neighbors like that. That remark he heard puzzled him. At twenty-eight dollars a head, the entire bunch couldn't have been worth more than three hundred dollars, and likely less.

The night was no longer friendly. It came to him that his own horses might have vanished the same way. He could not follow that bunch, not alone and unarmed. Later, before the tracks melted, perhaps. But even one day of chinook sun would destroy them, turn them into shapeless dimples of ice or destroy the snow altogether.

He rode tensely back to the Van Pelt ranch and pulled into the corrals before nine. The house was quiet and the fires were almost dead when he entered. She had slept on into the morning. Canada crumpled his note and threw it into the coals and then piled wood into the stove and fireplaces.

When the fireplaces were crackling, her door opened a crack. "I'm sorry I slept late," she smiled. "I was more tired than I realized. I'll be out in a minute and fix us some flapjacks."

He stared as the door eased shut, blanking the glimpse of her red hair and sleepy-warm lips.

He stalked savagely outside and forked

hay to the horses. He brushed the back of the mare until the saddle marks were gone, and the mare turned her head back to him, unsettled by his furious brushing.

"I'm living in a dreamworld that'll end when we get to Billings. The sooner the better!" he muttered angrily. "From now on I'll call her Mrs. Van Pelt, the way I should. Just as a reminder of who I am — and who she is."

She was flipping flapjacks when he came in, her crown of sorrel tied into a ponytail. He decided not to say anything about his discovery — not just yet. She had burdens enough, and he wanted some more information: the extent of the rustling and how many Van Pelt cattle were lost. But he also decided she should ride out with him and see with her own eyes what was happening.

"You're a sleepyhead, Mrs. Van Pelt," he joked. "I've already had my morning gallop."

She glanced at him, discovering something strange in his address and a new metallic tone in his voice. He seemed hard and cool, and she wondered if she had become a time-consuming burden that he resented.

"I'd like to ride today," she said softly. "Perhaps to your place so you can continue with your work. You must be eager to start training again."

"Oh, there's no rush," he said offhandedly. "Everything's gonna freeze up soon and then we can get you safely to Billings and on the train. Thought you'd like to ride out and look at your stock today."

"That'd be nice," she said absently.

"Tell me about those Herefords," he said. "Came from Nebraska?"

"Yes. Daddy bought them. They're supposed to be fine animals. Randy told me they grow to eleven hundred pounds in the time the longhorns take to reach seven hundred. . . . I guess there aren't very many in the West, and these are the first in Montana."

"What do they sell for?"

"Oh, I don't know. The same as other cattle I guess. Only Randy told me that he was going to sell the bulls in some special way — an auction I think. He said the better ones are worth a lot."

"How much?"

"Four or five hundred dollars, if he could find ranchers who understood what the bulls could do for their herds."

"Let's go have a look," Canada said with an urgency that surprised her.

She packed a saddlebag lunch, and then they were off, riding the chinook winds east.

He had only the mesa to guide him in that broken land, so he stuck to the ridge tops to keep it in sight.

Except for a big elk, they saw nothing all morning, and no cattle tracks. He realized she was a fine horsewoman, riding effortlessly beside him and never wearying.

"Were you going to try to handle a place this size all alone?" he asked.

"No. When spring came and the calving and the roundup, Randy was going to hire some cowboys. There's a bunkhouse for them. But we didn't really need them in the winter."

At the nooning he steered her up a long, grassy slope and into a niche in the cap rock where low tawny walls rose on three sides and the sun flooded in from the fourth. It was warm, and there was no wind. He unsaddled the mare and gelding and staked them on tender green grass that had sprouted next to the warm sandstone.

She shed her sheepskin, and Canada was instantly aware again of the thin, girlish figure moving angularly beneath the woolen shirt.

"Have a sandwich, Mrs. Van Pelt."

She gazed at him. "Why have you called me that all day?" she asked.

"Reminds me who I am," he said edgily.

"No. It reminds you who *I* am. Or who you think I am," she blazed. "I don't like it, Canada." A fire torched in her green eyes. "This isn't New York and there's no social register here. It takes strong men to build this country, and you're one of them. I'm not sure I could. You kept me from freezing to death."

She smiled, and he was abashed by her directness.

"That's part of it," he snapped. "Only part of it, Mrs. Van Pelt."

She surveyed him, and he couldn't return the gaze or meet the fire in her eye. And then suddenly awareness came to her and she softened, realizing at last her effect on him and how savagely he had trammeled his feelings.

"You're more a gentleman than any man I've met," she smiled softly. "Call me Mrs. Van Pelt then, Canada. You're quite right."

They found six Herefords that afternoon, and three early-bird calves at their sides. And that was all.

"We'll have an awful time finding them," she sighed. "Eight hundred, not including the new calves, and we found six after a whole day."

"I'll keep looking and send you a report. The news may not be so good," he said.

"A report?"

"Chinook's almost over," he said. "See those high streamers? I've been watching 'em move in from the north. Chinooks come out of the west. It'll freeze up hard tonight, so you'd better pack your trunks this evening and we'll take the buckboard tomorrow."

She sighed, suddenly aware of the long journey.

"Why do you think the news won't be good?" she asked.

"I think you're being rustled blind," he said.

She absorbed that quietly.

"I think Randy was coming to that conclusion before he . . . died. I guess we really were greenhorns out here."

"No," Canada replied, "rustlers clean out the toughest and savviest old ranchers in the territory. But I'll have to look into all this. Don't take me for gospel."

"Are we safe? Can't they come and, and kill us?" she asked nervously.

"No person's ever safe," he replied somberly. "I'm wearing this hogleg, that's all I can say. It's usually when we feel safest that the roof caves in."

She was glad when they turned into the ranch yard and reached the solid security of the log home.

Not long after first light of the bitter dawn, Canada had his cheerful mares harnessed and the buckboard at the door. The earth was not yet frozen hard, but the mud was stiff enough so that there'd be little trouble. He dragged two steamer trunks of her things across the frozen ground and then into the wagon, along with her valises. Then he added a barrel of her china.

He released the Van Pelt horses and propped the corral gates open. He left the windmill in gear so that it would lift water whenever the wind blew, regardless of what was in the galvanized tank in the corrals.

She came out then, bundled against the clawing cold, and paused. He sat quietly, holding the reins while she stared one last time at the place that had been her Eden. She excused herself and walked up the hill, her breath steaming in the gray air, and then disappeared from Canada's sight. He knew she was saying good-bye and that she had to do it alone. So he sat quietly, gloomily, while the cold bit his toes. She returned then, climbed beside him, and spread the buffalo robe across them both. He saw that she had wept. The first amber rays of sun caught the glistening wet upon her cheeks.

The mares were eager to be off, and they

danced forward to warm up, and the wagon rolled lightly behind. Three hours later they stopped at Canada's. He tossed out some hay while she brewed steaming tea. And then they were off again down the hard, bumpy road that led to Billings.

They rattled down the long slopes of the Bulls, through ponderosa that crowded close at times, and then they emerged out upon the high plains, where the ponderosa disappeared except for scraggly outriders.

Ahead was the great McFarland ranch, the 30-Mile, and as they dropped down into the prairie they could see wood smoke drifting south from the chimneys. Linda hadn't known the ranch existed, though she had passed it her first trip north.

"We'll pull in for coffee," Canada said. "It's the custom, and there may be something we can pick up for them in Billings. The McFarlands have one of the biggest spreads in Montana, maybe two hundred sections. Goes up to my little place, west about twenty miles, east some, and south most of the way to Billings."

He turned into the friendly ranch yard, almost surrounded by log sheds and pole corrals.

A short, red-faced man with sandy hair appeared on the wide veranda.

"Canada Parker, now you've gone and done it. Got you a right pretty bride, and you've come to show her off," he hollered.

"Not exactly," Canada retorted as he tugged gently on the reins. "This is Mrs. Van Pelt. Linda Van Pelt. She's been a neighbor all winter over at the old Buzhardt place, which they bought."

"By gawd, a pretty girl like you right over the hill; why, I'da lost all my crew if they knew, and maybe woulda lost me too," he joked.

Linda smiled thinly.

"Stuart —" Canada said edgily, "Mrs. Van Pelt lost her husband a few days ago. The grippe or pneumonia it was. I'm getting her on the train."

The rancher was embarrassed. "I'm sorry, Mrs. Van Pelt. Meant no offense. Hope you'll have a sip of coffee . . ."

Linda smiled. "Please," she begged, "please don't make a special case of me. I'd love to have coffee."

"Road's froze up so we can move," Canada explained. "She'll catch the morning eastbound. Anything I can getcha?"

"Let me consult Lollipop," Stuart replied. "Sit you down there and pour a cup."

"I hear Canada," — the sound came from the livingroom — "Canada, you old horse crippler, where've you been?"

Anne McFarland paused in the doorway and brushed back a strand of curly hair when she saw Linda.

"Oh! You brought company!"

Canada introduced Linda, explained her circumstance, and the wariness in Anne's face changed to sympathy. But Stuart McFarland's earthy daughter also saw in Canada's demeanor what few women could see: a burning pain in his eyes that sometimes seemed to crop out around his lips. She didn't know the cause of it; Canada always kept a certain distance, perhaps — she suspected — because he thought himself a failure.

The coffee slid down well on an icy morning, but Canada was restless. There were thirty miles to cover before dark.

"Got to go, Stuart. Road might still be muddy, and it'd take half your crew to pull me out."

"You'll be stuck then, Canada. They're all off hunting cows, 'cept Fireball. Blamed critters disappeared. They couldn't all have been winterkilled. We'd of found skeletons. Darned things probably drifted west somewhere, and the boys are lookin'."

"You too," said Canada metallically.

"What do you mean by that?" McFarland asked.

"Mrs. Van Pelt's missing most of her Herefords — purebred stock, by the way. Maybe seven hundred out of eight hundred they stocked the place with."

Awareness grew in McFarland's eyes.

"And I'm missing a dozen horses, including my Thoroughbred stallions. And maybe a few cows."

"And I'm short five or six hundred beeves," Stuart muttered grimly. "Anything you can point a finger at?"

"I think so, Stuart. But it'll need studying."

The old rancher sighed and ran a weathered hand through his unruly mane.

"Well, I can build a noose as good as the next man," he said slowly. "Done it before, too. Plenty of cottonwoods along the coulees. . . . What's her brand?" He nodded toward Linda.

"VP left thigh. Some older cows have a T-Bar. All Herefords."

"We'll be lookin'," McFarland grunted. "Want us to keep an eye on that place after you're gone, ma'm?"

"That would be very kind," Linda said. "My father would reimburse you, I'm sure."

"T'aint for money, it's for neighbors," Mc-

Farland retorted. "My good wishes ride with you then."

Linda blushed. The West was still eluding her.

The buckboard clattered south while the ruddy man and buxom daughter watched from their porch.

Canada and Linda rattled down the corrugated ruts, silver where the water had frozen. Once in a while the wagon squished through a soft place, or broke ice, but the going was easy in the cold.

Linda huddled under the buffalo robe and counted antelope, which grazed in white-rumped bunches. Canada was silent. In fact, he had mastered the desolation the twenty-two-year-old widow aroused in him, and was thinking about his missing horses.

"Why are you single, Canada?" she asked suddenly. "I could tell Anne McFarland is interested in you. I saw it in her. But you never paid her any attention . . ."

He said nothing for so long she wondered whether he was angry.

"Shy, I guess," he said carefully. "I almost did marry once. Anita."

"I'm sorry," she said. "I'd think you could offer a girl everything she'd want. You're strong, and you have something . . . a sense of honor, a code —"

He was growing embarrassed.

"And a long string of failures which I'm not blaming on anyone or anything but me," he shot back.

"That's your code, that's what I'm saying is so rare in you," she said. "Couldn't you like yourself a little more?"

He glared at her, and she slid back into silence, which remained unbroken until they rattled down into the Yellowstone Valley after dark, and he pulled up at the River Hotel on Montana Street, near the NP station.

He took her valises into the yellow board-and-batt building, thrown up hurriedly for railroad workers and travellers. They registered, and then rattled through the dark to the station, gloomy in the night. Linda bought her ticket and wired her family while Canada unloaded the trunks and barrel at the shipping office.

When they emerged from the rank air of the station into the frosty night, the rails glimmered with the light of a westbound train. Freight 53 arrived with a great screeching of brakes, hissing, and chuffing. Its carbide lamp flickered down the long, white rails and foul coal smoke lowered from its conical stack.

A man jumped from the cab and ran

toward the station.

"Where's the sheriff?" he cried. "Annie Armbruster's been shot! Gotta get help!"

He scurried inside, while Canada and Linda stared. They watched other men shuffle among the boxcars, lifting boxes, lowering sacks. And then, with a long wail that echoed through Canada's heart, Freight 53 chuffed to life and vanished in a cloud of steam.

The rails glistened cold and lonely in the white starlight. The tawny cliffs of the river valley loomed darkly north and south, encasing the tawdry little town in its own seclusion. Canada could barely stand the place.

They walked silently through the March night to the amber lights of the hotel, past a row of false-front buildings along the railroad street. There were blanketed Indians standing silently at corners and in front of saloons — Crow, Cheyenne, Sioux; and Canada eyed them warily: eight years had elapsed since the death of George Custer a few miles south, and some of those motionless figures had no doubt been present.

They ate silently in the sleazy dining room, and then Linda excused herself. Canada slept fitfully in the icy room so badly built that the night winds rustled his hair. He met her for breakfast and the sight of her melted him anew. She wore city clothes he hadn't seen, a gray woolen suit with a snowy starched collar that was encircled by a black velvet choker. There was a cameo of jade green at her throat, and the color matched her eyes. It was the clothing she was born to.

She understood his solemnness and didn't try to make light of it. They wore no false fronts in this false-front town. The eight o'clock train puffed in early, with the low eastern sun illumining the billowing white smoke of the enameled green engine.

"Thank you, Canada," she whispered at the steps of the snow-caked Pullman. "I needed your strength and kindness, all that you gave. I can't thank you enough. . . . God bless you always . . ."

She looked up at him, into his troubled gray eyes. Then she slipped a gloved hand up to the back of his neck and kissed him gently. And then she disappeared, mercifully to a compartment on the far side where he couldn't see her.

"Boaaaard," yelled the conductor as he swung up. The heavy flanged wheels rolled slowly, then faster, and in a moment there was nothing but a humming of the iron rails where he stood, remembering her kiss.

Chapter Four

Preacher Jonas stared through the gathering twilight into the Yellowstone River valley. Trees formed a black mass in the bottoms. Off to the west in the murky dusk was the yellow sandstone pillar where Lewis and Clark had carved their names early in the century — the only mementos of their epochal journey.

Preacher's pale eyes rested upon the hunkering settlement closer by, a dismal crossroads that boasted three houses, a false-front store, and a yellow board-and-batt train station hard by the Northern Pacific rails. The place existed for the stopping of trains. Orange light shone in the station window.

He was two days late. The chinook had stopped him. If he had moved the herd when the ground was soft, he would have left a trail any fool could follow back to the Bull Mountains. But the ground had frozen hard again, in this last spasm of winter, and what small trail he had left across the barren snow-patched hills would swiftly vanish.

Preacher had ridden the whole day and half the previous night. He had timed the drive to reach here exactly now, as the dark thickened. He didn't want prying eyes to see the fresh brands on those Herefords. They were the only purebreds that he knew of in Montana, and he could no more hide them than he could hide a parade of elephants. And it wouldn't take a savvy rancher long to see how a running iron had embellished the VP brands into a Diamond B, and an X Ladder.

The boxcars. That clerk in Billings, who got a double eagle for his pains, had waybilled them to the Pompeys Pillar siding for a whole week. Preacher drew his pocket watch. It was five-thirty now, plenty of time to load for the seven-twenty westbound.

Preacher was bone-tired. They all were, after a day and a half's drive down the long swales of the plains as they dropped toward the swift river.

"I'm going in to check it out," Preacher said quietly to Yuma. "You an' Wichita and Scorch follow along in a bit, when it's darker, and put the bulls in the pens. Then we'll load and get out."

The wiry man with the jet-black hair and pointy beard nodded and turned his gelding back around the muttering animals to tell the others. Preacher spurred his handsome quarter gelding — he was fond of good horseflesh — down the long slope and into the owly town, not liking the place at all. Something about it made his flesh crawl.

The north wind rattled an outhouse door and made the telegraph wires whine. A window shivered and bulky tumbleweeds rolled in front of his bay, spooking it. A desolate place on a desolate night.

It was black when Preacher reached the siding.

There were no boxcars.

Anger stormed up in him, and manic suspicion. There should have been four. Was it a mistake? A trap? He resisted the urge to turn and run. "The wicked flee when no man pursueth," he said to himself. It was a verse he knew well, from a boyhood spent assisting his circuit-riding father in camp-town revivals.

The ball was high on the signal pole. The freight would highball through unless he lowered it. He spurred the gelding gently to the station hitch rail, eased off, and stretched his skinny legs after their long, cold imprisonment in the saddle. Behind the blurry window he saw someone.

He was greeted with the chatter of the telegraph key. Through the grilled ticket window he saw a woman in the lamplight, her fingers racing Morse into the wires.

She turned and rose when she was finished. She was tall, maybe even six feet, with a man's shoulders, lantern jaw, and half-closed eyes.

"I'm looking for Armbruster," he said slowly.

"I'm Armbruster."

"I didn't expect —"

"My man and I, we run it together," she rumbled. "Take turns. He's over yonder at the house. . . . What do you want?"

He smiled ingratiatingly, a tall man with a beak nose, gray hair that was once blond, pale eyes that focused on her forehead, her cheeks, her mouth, but never met her stare.

"I'm from the Diamond B, up near Grass Range, and we've been driving cattle three days. There were supposed to be boxcars for us here, ready for the westbound, Number 53, I think, any time this week."

Her eyes opened a bit. "I sent 'em out yesterday. Some cater-wumpus in Billings."

"Oh? Some sort of trouble?" he asked casually.

She stared at him from beneath her droop-

71

ing eyelids.

"Makes no difference," she said. "You pen your cattle over at the ramp now and I'll wire for cars, and they'll be dropped in the morning. You'll ship tomorrow."

"How about tonight?" he asked. "Any empties on that freight?"

"I can't hold it more than ten minutes even if they was," she replied.

"It's only a hundred bulls and bull calves."

"Why tonight? What's your rush? You've traveled three days? I've never heard of shipping only bulls," she said irritably.

"God helps those who help themselves, Mrs. Armbruster. I'll go drop that ball and you write up the waybill. Diamond B, Grass Range, consignor. Barnstable, Nugent, River Pass, Oregon, consignee."

"No," she said.

He stared narrowly at the angular woman, an unbudging bureaucratic force in her barren cubicle.

"Well," he said cheerfully, " 'What you sow, so shall you reap,' according to the Good Book. I like to reward good service. Make a point of it, in fact. Good business. Builds trust. The man who is generous in business, why, the Good Lord always prospers him . . ."

"I don't accept tips — if that's the word

for it," she rumbled. "And I don't trust you. You're a smiling type that talks gospel and smells like a crook, with your tied-down pistol like the wild bunch. What's a matter with those bulls? Brands a little too fresh for daylight? Now you get outa here before I get my man."

Her black eyes bored through Preacher mercilessly in the gathering silence.

"Grass Range, my foot," she snorted. "It's a shorter drive to Billings. And there's thirty miles less tariff westbound."

Almost before Preacher comprehended, she had a double-barreled shotgun on him, and he stared down two black twelve-gauge holes.

"Now you drop that hogleg slowlike before I cut you in two. We're a-goin' to my man."

Preacher cursed wildly inside himself, and eased his hands slowly to the tiedown thongs and undid them. Then slowly up toward his belt buckle.

Wichita entered in a blast of icy air, slammed the station door, and absorbed the sight of the leveled shotgun ten feet away, even as its barrel swung toward him. He dug for his Colt, but the shotgun exploded deafeningly in the tiny wooden room, and all nine of the double-ought buckshot ripped into his chest.

Preacher jammed his hand down smoothly and drilled a .44 slug at the woman, even as her second blast whipped by, with one ball plucking his coat. She dropped wordlessly, a blue hole in her forehead, and the shotgun clattered to the plank floor. The stink of powder smoke drifted past the kerosene lamp.

Preacher paused, paralyzed at the grisly sights. Wichita's face leered at him. He heard a slamming door outside, and a man running. Methodically Preacher leveled his pistol at the telegraph key and shattered it with one shot, then blasted the spare key with another. A third blew the wick off the lantern, plunging the station into gloom. Then he bolted into the night, sprang upon his bay, fired his last rounds at the running man, and spurred the gelding savagely west along the roadbed.

He heard other horses running. Scorch and Yuma. No one at the crossroads had time to saddle.

A rifle boomed behind, snarling lead and vengeance. Preacher went raggedy with fear, and his jaded bay stumbled in the gloom.

The bulks of two horsemen drew up to him, scrambling through the mad night.

"Where's Wichita?" Scorch yelled.

"Dead. Woman blew him apart. She's

dead," Preacher snarled back. "Where's those bulls?"

"In the pen, like you said, sir," Yuma mumbled.

"The Lord gives and the Lord takes away," Preacher babbled, wanting to go back for them. Those hundred bulls, priceless broodstock for western herds, would have brought $25,000.

Yuma smiled in the dark, unseen.

They reined up at the very base of Pompeys Pillar and let the weary horses blow.

"I shot out the telegraph. They ain't going to be on our trail till tomorrow, when they scratch up a posse," Preacher announced philosophically.

"Wichita dead? Oh, hell," Scorch muttered dismally.

"The Good Lord come and took him up in the station house," intoned Preacher.

"She done him a favor," Yuma added.

Preacher shucked his empties and filled the army Colt with fresh .44s, using the ritual to pull himself together.

"Ground's frozen so we won't leave sign. Horses are done in. But no one's coming tonight. We can walk away."

He slumped in the saddle, punchy. The implications began to seep through him as they walked quietly into the bitter north wind. The Herefords would be discovered, the phony brands spotted. He could never ship from here again. A fast posse could track those bulls to the mountains tomorrow. Those rich Van Pelts would likely spend a mint to solve the crime. The NP would, too. It had to be a woman. That was a necktie party for certain.

Preacher smiled. When things were that black, they were usually pretty good if a man had faith. Why, any fool posse that'd try to thread through those Bull Mountains would get lost, or maybe shot at some from the cap rock.

"I'm ridin' to Roundup for some refreshments at Grizzly Bear's," he yawned. "I'm going to have a look-see at the Van Pelt place on the way, and maybe bother Pike and Maudie some so they won't go blabbing to some posse."

Scorch didn't like it. "I think we should split up. Then they'd never git a one of us," he said sullenly. "I'm fixin' to go on down to Hole in the Wall, and stay with the bunch until things cool down."

Preacher's gray eyes bored sadly into the lanky night rider.

"I don't think so," he said silkily. "You just haven't got faith, Scorch. The Book says, 'If a man has faith he can move mountains.' Why, we've still got fifteen hundred critters stashed around Pike and Maudie's."

"I'm sick of you and your damned book."

"Ah, Scorch, trouble is, you never think of others. Only saving your own skin, leavin' Yuma and me alone. Remember the golden rule, do unto others —"

Yuma smiled, watching the cold blue glint in Preacher's hand.

"You're crazy, Preacher, and you got us into a fix. I'm getting the hell out," Scorch snapped.

"Now that's loyalty for you, son. Here I gave you fifty and found, fightin' wages, just to do some artwork with that hot iron of yours, twenty more than you could get from any other outfit." Preacher sighed. "Now you leave us in our travail. Well, go along, son. Leave the flock."

"You mean I kin go?"

"You'll do yourself a favor," chimed in Yuma.

Preacher nodded solemnly. Scorch trotted off fast into the darkness, his spine tingling. Preacher gave him two seconds, raised his Colt, and drilled him through the back. The blast rattled into the night, clattering through the icy hills. Scorch slumped, and then thudded into the frozen ground; he coughed once and died.

"Get the horse, Yuma," Preacher mumbled. "We may need a spare. Poor devil made the mistake of picking bad company. Why, that wild bunch over yonder of the Big Horns, they're all scum. Not a one of them a decent man would want to be seen with. I wouldn't want a one upon the ranch I'm a-building, lest they destroy my good name."

"You did him a favor, sir," Yuma said quietly. "Some men are better off dead."

Yuma had done favors for many a man in his day. When he was a Confederate major he had done the favor to seven cowards running from battle. He did the favor to fourteen Union prisoners who faced misery and starvation. As a guard at the Arizona Territorial Prison, he had done the favor to several lifers, hopeless men.

"Lots of scum in the West, sir," Yuma agreed. "Bringing dishonor upon themselves, and misery."

They trotted through the nippy night, then walked their stumbling mounts, rotating the spare horse, numb to the marrow. By dawn they were threading into the valleys of the Bulls, leaving no trail at all on the stiff ground. Their energies ebbed low.

The geldings couldn't be prodded. Preacher began to look back frequently as the light intensified. He couldn't help it. But they were alone.

"Providence has placed us close to the Van Pelt ranch," Preacher said. "Two weary pilgrims, seeking breakfast and a good job."

Yuma smiled as he slid down from the saddle. Pain knifed up through his numb legs.

"Thirty and found," he agreed. "A fair wage for two saddle tramps riding the line."

They walked gamely ahead, scarcely noticing the beauty of the golden grass against the forested slopes. It was country they knew well, country where Herefords had roamed.

"Where better to weather storms than in the bosom of our upright neighbors?" Preacher asked.

"Where are we from?" Yuma inquired.

"Why, always tell the truth, man," Preacher responded. "Don't you know that liars need good memories? Are we not two laddies from Wyoming, riding the line, loyal to whatever brand hires us on?"

"Indeed we are," Yuma agreed.

"Take courage, my man, for I have distilled certain principles of conduct from the Good Book, pressed upon me by my late reverend

79

father, bless his soul, and may he rest in peace."

"I know them exactly," Yuma said. "Mother's milk, sir."

They trudged wearily up the ranch road and stood at last in the yard, hushed in the morning sun. No smoke. No horses in the corrals. The windmill creaked lazily.

"I do believe they are not about. This sterling place, the ruby of the Bull Mountains, has been dropped into our needful laps. . . . Let's try the door," Preacher said, gazing piously upon the buildings.

No one answered. They grained and hayed the horses and let themselves into the solid log home, which was cold as a mausoleum within.

"In Billings, perhaps. Certainly not abandoned. Our neighbors have left furnishings, goods, and chattels," proclaimed Preacher. "Build a fire, Yuma, and we'll borrow some of that oatmeal for a hearty breakfast."

They ate greedily in the circle of the creeping warmth from the kitchen range. Then they explored the home thoroughly.

"Only men's clothes here. No woman's," said Yuma, with some curious disappointment. "Not even a petticoat. She must be far away, traveling."

"Ah, Yuma. I've heard tell she's beautiful.

80

What a pity." Preacher exclaimed.

"A pity, sir?"

"That we cannot have her, along with the rest of this establishment, Yuma. But I shall have faith. Perhaps she, too, will yield like succulent fruit."

They rested through the morning, while the horses restored their energies for the last lap.

"Time flies, Yuma. Touch nothing here. Clean up everything. Leave no trace. The Van Pelts have been most hospitable to us, and we shall apply the golden rule, and leave them no messes."

"Or evidence," Yuma said softly.

They rode leisurely north in the midday sun, along an owlhoot trail, over steep ridges capped with grotesque wind-carved sandstone. Down through copses of juniper. Through deep glades of ponderosa. Out upon golden grassy bowls. Past little herds of longhorns bearing the brands of Ezekiel Earley to the east, Cicero Billington to the north, and the McFarlands to the south. It was a tumbled land, no place for sojourners, but a country that could hide armies.

"That Van Pelt place. Now, there's a majestic ranch, to my eye. Lying in the heart of these hills," Preacher rhapsodized. "Clean, solid, good grass and water. Everything mended and in shape. A place to put down roots, marry. Here I am, already gray, and wifeless. And no flesh of my flesh to bless me until the Chariot comes for me."

Yuma grinned.

"Rustlers. The wild bunch. They don't live long, Yuma. Usually stretch a rope before they're thirty. All that riffraff think they can get away with it. You and I, now, we know better. You're thirty-six, a retired brevet major for the South, a gentleman bred. Didn't you tell me Harkness was your proper name? You and I, now, after we get the Van Pelt place we'll keep the riffraff off."

"You know," countered Yuma, "if a fella owned that Van Pelt place he could just about hold off an army in that country. A few hardcases guarding the passes, and you'd be a law unto yourself."

"No. I'd join the Cattlemen's Protective Association that is being organized over yonder at Gilt Edge by Granville Stuart. There's no future in sin, Yuma."

Yuma sighed. "A man could control these Bulls so complete he'd never have to ship beeves with phony brands. He could just sort of borry neighborin' cows, keep 'em safe up here, and keep the calves. Put his own iron on the weanlings and slip the mammies back to their home spreads. A place like this, why a dozen hardcases would seal it tighter than a dead man's mouth."

"Shame on you, Yuma, thinking evil thoughts," snapped Preacher. "Think good thoughts. The Good Lord is about to deliver us the Van Pelt place, all respectable and bought for a fair price."

"There's plenty of hardcases up at Grizzly Bear's that we could hire," Yuma persisted. "They'd come aboard for gun-carryin' wages, fifty and found."

"The wages of sin is death." Preacher intoned it with a sepulchral authority.

"Sure, when you're eighty," the bantam retorted. "In the meantime, you could get the whole Bull Mountains and maybe that bouncy McFarland girl you keep thinkin' about."

"Get thee behind me, Satan," growled Preacher, a thin grin spreading across his gray face.

They splashed into the yard of a decaying hardscrabble nester ranch set bleakly on a bare slope, and drew up before a slatternly log house moldering in the spring slop.

Preacher yanked at the kitchen door — it was hanging from one hinge — and glared irritably into a filthy kitchen piled with greasy dishes and putrefied slobbers of food.

"Maudie, how about some eats? And on

clean plates, dammit, before you poison us."

"Fend for yourselves. I ain't started anything," muttered an ancient woman with a vast belly as she shuffled in. "I ain't feeling well today."

"Of course you aren't," Preacher agreed. "Not after a quart of bourbon." He smiled sympathetically. "The Good Book, it says that drunkards can't enter the kingdom. Where's Pike?"

"Right here," yawned Pike Sanders, scratching his crotch. He was lumpy, bald, and pig-eyed. There was a five-day growth of beard scraggling his jowls.

"Pike, if you don't get this slatherass outfit fixed up, you'll never get a dime out of me," Preacher scolded. "Those corrals need fixin'. How am I supposed to keep my cattle in them? You'd better nail up some poles if you want your pasture money."

"I've been busy," Pike whined. "I can't get all that nailed up at once. Sun sets early these days."

"The Lord helps those who help themselves, Pike," Preacher said.

Pike drew himself up stiffly. "It's my place to do with as I want. You pay me first, then maybe I'll get the corrals nailed up."

Preacher stared sourly at the lumpy nester. "The Good Book says," he proclaimed, "that those who don't work, don't eat."

Yuma grinned.

"Pike, you're on the road to perdition. You're too lazy to shave. Too lazy to put your boots on, even though you've got holes in those socks and your feet's cold. And you've got a month's groceries dribbling down your sweater."

"Aw, quit pickin' on the old man," snarled Maudie.

Preacher shook his head sadly, a man in sorrow. "The outhouse stinks because you're too lazy to lime it. The well hardly pumps because you never change the leathers. Those windows stayed broke all winter. The stoves are so full of ashes they hardly hold a fire. Two doors are off their hinges. Your mares aren't shod. Barn roof's caved in. Wagon tongue busted. Pike, you'll have to re-pent. Get down on your knees and re-pent. Start livin' the new life."

"I've been busy planning," Pike retorted confidently. "I've got her all figured out, what to do. No sense wasting labor and having to redo everything. Planning's hard work, to stay progressive and all that."

"How are my cattle doin'?" Preacher asked abruptly.

"How should I know? I ain't been out there. That's your job. You're the one renting," Pike replied loftily. "Say, where are those others, Wichita and Scorch?"

"They had some bad luck down near Pompeys Pillar. Got in with some rustlers, I'm told, and got themselves killed. There's a posse out a-hunting."

"Killed?" Pike blanched.

"That's what I heard," said Preacher. "Plumb dead. Now if that posse comes, you tell 'em we're all God-fearin' people here."

"Why would a posse come here?" Pike demanded.

"Probably won't," Preacher soothed. "And anyway, they can tell an upright man good as the next one. It's those hardcases they want."

Yuma was amused.

"Well, I'm as honest as anyone else," Pike muttered. "Trouble is, taxes eat me up. The minute I improve something, they take it away in taxes. There's just no reason to improve a place if'n the county's gointa get it. It's just theft."

It didn't really matter, Preacher thought. Soon he'd be done with the scruffy outfit. Done with dirt and nesters. He had rustled the Van Pelts out of everything they had on grass; it wouldn't take long now for them to pull out. Maybe they already had.

Preacher grinned. He still had over six

hundred of the VP Herefords scattered through obscure valleys of this outfit. All of them gold mines. All Diamond B or X Ladder now. And the other cattle, old Texas-style longhorns, nine hundred strong, stashed away round and about. As soon as he got the VP, he'd move most of 'em.

"Pike," said Preacher dolefully, "if you don't clean those stovepipes, you'll have a chimney fire that'll burn you out one of these days."

"Been meanin' to," Pike remembered. "But it's almost spring. And anyway, I'm just too busy running this big operation. I ain't got time for petty things."

"Well, I hope you and Maudie don't get burned up one of these nights," Preacher sighed.

"It'd be a favor," Yuma mumbled.

"Brother Yuma, it's time we paid a neighborly visit on those Van Pelts down yonder. I'm a thinking we ought to offer to rent pasture from them."

"You can't do that, you're rentin' from me," Pike whined.

"Pike, friend, you just don't keep up the fences and corrals like you should. How can I run cattle? It makes it twice as hard for me to ranch."

"Pay me, and I'll repair," Pike grumbled.

"You haven't given us a damn dime," Maudie snarled. "Maybe you should get your thievin' tail off our land."

"You sorrow me, brother, sorrow me," Preacher intoned. "The Good Book says, owe no man anything and that's the way I live. I'll settle in gold soon enough. Brother Yuma, let's saddle some horses."

They didn't ride to the VP. They rode to Grizzly Bear Polarski's saloon, hard by the Musselshell, to do some hiring of a few select men with certain capabilities.

CHAPTER FIVE

Canada watched the distant stranger open the gate, drive a light wagon through, and carefully close it.

He touched the flanks of Crowbait and loped him again around the perimeter of the long slabwood corral.

"You haven't been ridden for a time and you show it, lazybones," he muttered affectionately to the sweating sorrel gelding. Crowbait was in his prime, and not for sale.

He tied the horse and stood waiting in the stingy March sun for the stranger in the black suit who was driving a pair of dappled grays up the long grade.

The man, sallow from indoor work, drew up before Canada and quietly surveyed the whole lay of the place with eyes that missed nothing and reflected responsibility.

"It's good to get out. I've been looking for a chance to bust loose from my office for days. You're Parker?"

"I am," Canada nodded.

"Put this place together all yourself, no help?"

"It's temporary," Canada apologized. "I couldn't take time away from horse training. Now, what can I do for you?"

"On the frontier, the temporary must serve until we can build better," said the man amiably. "I'm Thomas Bell, with the NP."

Canada nodded. "I thought perhaps someone like you might come along. How's Mrs. Van Pelt? Safe back there in New York?" The name sobered him and renewed a hollowness that had haunted him all week.

"She is. And grateful to you for your assistance during her bereavement and distress."

Canada grinned suddenly. "Well, don't just stand there. Come in and have some coffee — it's black enough to curl the hair on your chest. I'll grain your team; you've come a long piece."

It was obvious to Bell that the gaunt young man had a way with horses. Parker's own stock was remarkable for its strength and beauty on a frontier where most men settled for broomtail mustangs or hammerhead Indian ponies.

"The Reeds — that's Mrs. Van Pelt's family — don't quite know what to do with the ranch," Bell began after they had settled down on the warm front stoop. "Especially with the rustling. You know anything about that?"

"I do," Canada said. "I figured it when I was helping Linda — Mrs. Van Pelt. She's not the only one hereabouts: we've all lost some. When I was down putting her on the eastbound, I heard tell of the business at Pompeys Pillar. Those were VP bulls."

Bell nodded. "Mrs. Armbruster was one of our best station-masters. Armbruster himself is grieving so much we've given him leave for a month. Sad business, and one the NP intends to remedy."

"I'm afraid Mrs. Van Pelt has lost seventy or eighty per cent of those Herefords. Maybe the rest, too, by now," Canada added, somberly.

"We've got the hundred VP bulls the rustlers abandoned," Bell said. "Their brands were altered to Diamond B and X Ladder. Neither brand is recorded."

Canada stood restlessly and pitched the dregs from his cup. The Big Sad, that was his private name for the relentless emotion that hamstrung his life. It was heavy on him now.

"You've driven thirty-five miles for some

sort of business, I'll wager," he said, unsmiling.

Bell eyed him thoughtfully. "I have a telegram for you from Mrs. Van Pelt's father. And I've also had considerable wire correspondence with him myself."

He handed the yellow sheet to Canada:

Mrs. Van Pelt and families eternally grateful to you for assistance rendered during her distress. Would you consider move to VP ranch with your stock at 50 dollars a month until its sale or disposal? Request early reply.

James P. Reed

Canada stared at the hills he loved; the hardscrabble ranch he called his own, and sighed. The vision of Linda, sorrel-haired, angular, and desirable in the winter sun, flooded through him.

Bell watched the changing feelings reflect themselves in Canada's features.

"Hard to pull up stakes, delay your own plans, work for someone else, isn't it?" he said softly.

"I'm not much good workin' for others," said Canada unhappily. "I always rile 'em up. But I'll go. Least I can do for her. I have some things in mind over there anyway."

"Such as?"

"Some quiet moseying around in the backcountry. I want to know where that stock went, and who's doing it."

"That's a fast way to die," said Bell quietly. "I don't think you're a hand with a gun."

"Shot a few rattlesnakes" — Canada grinned — "and a horse that busted his leg. Almost made me lose my grub, doin' that."

"Well, it's up to you. Mrs. Van Pelt is thinking of keeping the place. The country seems to agree with her. Reed is discouraging it and figures she'll get back into her old life again. An attractive girl like that won't be a widow long."

Something clutched at Canada, fear and hope all at once.

"She might be coming back?"

Bell laughed. "She probably needs to, just to get it out of her system. The West and its hardships will look a lot different to her without the romantic honeymoon. At any rate, if you accept, I'll wire Reed and have my men drive the VP bulls up here again. If not, we'll sell the bulls at auction. They'll fetch a fancy price out here."

"I'll accept."

"Good. I have your first month's pay in gold. And I'm authorized to approve any unusual expenses — windmill repair or the like. We'll be freighting up some grain and hay."

He dropped three double eagles into Canada's hand. "The ten is for supplies," he said.

Canada stared at the glinting gold in his palm. Bought. Bought for a month.

"I'd prefer to help for nothing," he muttered. "I don't like to take wages."

Bell looked at him oddly, in fact admiring the gray-eyed horseman. But Canada took it differently.

"Are you planning to stay over? Your standardbreds look tired," Canada said irritably.

"No, I've some business with the McFarlands and I'll stay at the 30-Mile. They're shipping soon."

Canada watched him go, the wagon leaving narrow furrows in the soft spring dirt. Some crabbing anger out of nowhere clawed at his insides and wouldn't let go. He leaped aboard Crowbait and tickled the big sorrel into an easy lope until he spotted the mares out in the hay meadow, and a band of gelded two-year-olds over the next hill. He drove them all down to the pens, and had a time of it because they were frisky in the spring sun.

The next morning he drove twenty-seven

94

horses to the VP. They were all he could find out of the sixty he owned, and none of his stallions was among them. It was a hard trip for a lone rider. The band was unruly, and Canada exhausted Crowbait chasing after laggards and quitters.

He penned them in the commodious VP pole corrals, hayed them well, and walked his weary gelding the nine miles back to his cabin in the chilly dusk. The next day he loaded his buckboard, backed his driving mares into the traces, tied Crowbait behind, and abandoned the little homestead where he had eked out a living for four years.

It was building toward a spring deluge when he pulled into the VP. The horses were restless and hungry. He hayed them first, while the skies lowered down to the hilltops and the light grayed down to gloom. The squall hit as he was unloading the buckboard.

He raced his food, clothes, and shotgun into the cold house, heaping it all on the planks. Then he unharnessed the mares in the soaking, cold gusts, and was bone-cold before he was done. Hail rattled the roof by the time he got in, and there was no warm stove to dry him.

A grudging fire warmed him at last, but he was unhappy. The place contained too many memories of Linda. He saw her in the kitchen, or peering from her bedroom door, her face soft with sleep. He saw her sitting in the wing chair, eyes wet with grief. He saw her standing at the southern window, her cheeks wet. He saw her shivering in the thin navy-blue shirtwaist after they had buried Randall Van Pelt.

He stared moodily at the heap of his shabby goods amidst these new, comfortable furnishings. The hail slowed, and the sky lightened. He couldn't stand the haunting house another minute and stormed out to the bunkhouse. It was peaceful there, full of male smells. There was a cookstove at the rear; bunks up front. And yet . . . it didn't suit him either. Never had he felt so orphaned.

Canada splashed slowly across the yard, deciding at last to stay in the log home and make peace with his memories. He was not a man to run away from the unbearable. He had lived with the unbearable since he was orphaned at fourteen, and he could take whatever life dished out. There was more courage in him than he knew, and more readiness to love than he understood. He settled in.

The next day, with a sky full of puffballs, he loaded his saddlebags, tied a yellow slicker over the cantle, and set off on Crow-bait to check the wells and track down the VP Herefords. His plan was simple enough: he would survey the whole ranch first, study sign, and then explore beyond the VP in the mountain country to the north.

The ranch was empty. There were deer and the fresh trail of an elk. But not a single cloven hoofprint of a cow. He explored the southern sections first. The windmill tanks were overflowing, and there were no prints in the mud.

Crowbait enjoyed the outings, and was tireless and adept in rough country. Canada pushed the gelding up tortuous trails, and in places the horse had to leap up rock shelves, or jump gullies. Canada backed the eager horse around tight corners, threaded him through snagging thickets, led him into dark defiles and down hidden coulees where the sandstone pressed so close that his stirrups clattered against the yellow rock.

The horse learned to hunt. Canada taught it to freeze at the press of a finger at the withers. They paused in shadow at the passage of a buck. Stopped quietly in the middle of a pasture for no reason other than that Canada had commanded it and he had obeyed.

Canada memorized the land, thinking

ahead to the possibilities of chase or refuge if he had to tangle with the cattle thieves. Here was a useful thicket; up there was a hideaway in the cap rock. Over yonder was a cutoff, over what seemed an impossible ridge.

He found two of the brown-and-white cows one day with a month-old calf. Missed by the rustlers, which could easily happen in this country. He herded them back to a pasture just below the VP headquarters, Crowbait making rowdy sport of it.

He rode some younger geldings, too, as he explored northward systematically, gradually covering the forty rugged sections of the VP. Canada was patient with the green colts, preferring to teach by repetition rather than rebuke. There were times he laid a crop to them, but such was his canny skill that they usually did his bidding without coercion.

By the end of April he had found less than fifty VP Herefords and had combed the ranch to his satisfaction. He moved them to pastures close to the big log house he called home, where they mingled with the bulls that Bell had sent back. He reported regularly to the NP officer, and regularly received sealed instructions and pay from the driver of the Roundup-Billings stage.

It was time to probe northward into country more mountainous and obscure, country two or three days' ride away. That meant leaving the ranch unattended a week at a time, but it couldn't be helped. He felt fairly certain he would find rustled cattle up there, unless they had been driven clean out of the country to the Missouri Breaks. But he doubted that. These Bull Mountains provided all the cover a cattle ring would ever need.

He dreaded the longer trips. The serene ranch had grown upon him as it did upon every person who ever had commerce with it. He knew danger lurked wherever the rustled cattle grazed; they would not be unguarded.

He started north on Crowbait and led one of his best young geldings, Payday, a black that would carry his packsaddle. He was outfitted for a week. He carried a pump-action shotgun and his hogleg, but he knew dismally that he had no chance at all against fast hardcases or bushwackers.

Payday would make a good night horse. Surefooted and quiet, unlikely to whinny the way a gregarious mare would if she smelled any of her race. Geldings had the advantage in work like this, he thought.

"Come along, Crowbait," he said aloud.

"It's time to ante up some big chips."

When at last he left the VP range, he walked warily, sticking to forested slopes where the shadow ran deep. The tumultuous hills lined out into ridges and the watercourses grew clearer and more predictable. He stayed clear of the valley floors where a traveler would be visible from any surrounding ridge. He stayed high, but never topped a ridge until he had dismounted and bellied up to the crest for a look downslope.

Late that afternoon, a dozen miles northwest of the VP line by his reckoning, he topped a ridge and found himself staring at a herd of eighty or a hundred longhorns. He was too high to read the brands; it would be foolhardy to go down there in broad daylight. He saw a small spring on the far slope, the type that often dried out in July or August in this country. He would water his horses there after dark.

He found a level spot in some high rimrock; the start of a crevasse that tumbled into a steep coulee. It was well concealed; a small fire there would not be seen from higher ground, and overhanging ledges would dissipate the smoke. He picketed the horses in a rocky pocket and quietly studied the country as twilight deepened. In one westward valley he saw the shapes of more cattle, blurs in the dusk.

He studied escape routes, cliffs, and slopes. His best hope, in trouble, would be to take these well-trained geldings straight over palisaded ridges if he could.

He heated some beans and bacon. When the stars were sharp in the deep, he led the geldings down to the seep across the meadow, and let them forage for an hour on the spring grass while he slipped silently among the cattle. He had trouble reading the brands, but after a patient half hour among the skittish cows he knew he could tell Stuart McFarland where some of his missing 30-brand cows were. The brands were not altered, and that suggested to Canada that the rustlers felt secure here, if not cocky.

He slept fitfully, not liking the hard ground and having little taste for manhunting and range policing. But the hope that he might uncover his own missing horses, as well as Linda's Herefords, spurred him on.

The next day, tired and trigger-tense, he worked north toward Roundup, a shadowy figure edging through ponderosa groves where russet needle carpets softened his sound and left not a hint of his passage.

Each valley here contained a small herd;

longhorns at first, but then, at last, one that pocketed forty or so Hereford steers. In one valley the forest stopped abruptly at a meadow, beside a coulee. He tied his horses and slid down until he was able to see the E Lazy E on some near longhorns. They belonged to old Ezekiel Earley who ranched along the Musselshell, to the northeast.

Canada kept a tally. By midafternoon he had counted four hundred animals, and had seen every major brand in central Montana. The Bull Mountains were a giant holding pen for a rustling ring so large that the thefts seemed inconceivable.

An hour later he cut the trail of a shod horse. The print was shiny, without any drying or decay. An hour or two old. Heading north along a faint owlhoot trail. Canada studied the tracks carefully, listening closely. Then he painfully tamped away his own sign and scattered pine debris over his prints. It wouldn't fool an Indian, but it might suffice here. The lone horseman might not have been alone; others might be coming. The thought made him prickle, and he redoubled his caution.

He began to discern a pattern. The cattle were never in the main thoroughfare valleys, the ones that drained the country and formed natural travel routes. It would be possible for a pilgrim traveling through this country never to see a beeve at all. Human travelers, like the four-footed ones, instinctively take the easiest trail and usually the levelest.

Canada feared the primary valleys, and when he had to cross one he chose a narrow point and studied it carefully before he ventured out.

Crowbait's ears perked, and the gelding turned his head to the right, nickering softly.

"Okay, boy, what is it?" Canada asked softly, already knowing. He turned the sorrel east, into a shallow watercourse that catapulted steeply up a ridge. The horse leaped from ledge to ledge while the black lunged along behind, bearing the deadweight of the pack. They topped out on a high cap that overlooked an alpine park of twenty or thirty acres, entirely surrounded by palisades of yellow stone. He saw his own horses in there, or at least some of them. The Thoroughbred stallion. The mares, yearlings, and some new foals he'd never seen. They stared up at him in the late sun.

The gelding nickered again, excited.

"Whoa, boy. You'll tangle with that stud if we're not careful. Beats me how you smelled 'em from the other side of the mountain." Canada was infinitely pleased.

He ground-tied the horses in a juniper patch, studied the palisades for a while, and then slipped out into the grassy park, whistling softly a four-note tune that all his horses knew. They stood watching, a hundred yards distant; then trotted, and finally loped up to him, milling about their old friend and master.

Canada laughed. He scratched jaws, petted noses, tugged ears, and slapped the pushy stallion back. The foals bleated and he looked them over as he roughhoused with the yearlings at this family reunion.

He felt the whip of lead as it tugged his hat before he heard the crack of a rifle. For a paralyzed moment he didn't understand. The second shot thumped into a yearling just in front of him; it coughed and sagged pitifully. The third and fourth shots snarled past him as he ran in terror toward the junipers. The fifth whined off of sandstone two feet to his right. There were others, but he didn't know where they struck.

He rounded a corner into safety, leaped up on Crowbait, and bolted into the fissured rock with Payday trotting serenely behind. He was momentarily safe inside the broken palisade.

Shaking uncontrollably, he realized he was on a fool's mission, and that he would very likely never see the VP ranch, or his own, again.

Bell had been right.

CHAPTER SIX

Canada paused in the shadowed fissure. It was quiet except for the tumult of his pulse. The tawny sandstone proffered safety; if he clattered down the slope below the palisades, he would probably be killed.

This was the first time he had ever been shot at. He had survived, and that surprised him. Once he had drawn his hogleg on some Crow Indians who coveted his horses, but that was his sole experience with guns. He was no tenderfoot after a life on the frontier, either.

He stood silently, not knowing what else to do. The horses were restless on the steep pitch, but he bid them to be quiet. He slid off Crowbait and eased slowly back up the defile with his old navy cap-and-ball drawn. He feared the drygulcher might simply crawl to the lip above him and shoot down.

It was growing dusky. Slowly he peered around rock until the high park came into view. Nothing. He looked for a sign of anything. Movement. A flash of metal.

Nothing. The horses grazed peacefully and were not staring in any direction. The dark bulk of the dead yearling was humped up in the grass and grieved Canada. In the gloom, taking great care with gravel, he crawled up to the top of the palisades, onto cap rock gray with lichen. One horse heard him and stared; the others grazed. Canada crawled toward the area the shots had come from, seeing no one. He was high; the view off the other side was a jumble of ridges in the dusk. A wavering light in the nearest valley, below, caught his eye, and he gradually made out the shape of a tumbledown ranch with a caved-in barn and collapsed corrals.

He had heard tell of a ranch up here, owned by some nesters named Sanders. There were plenty of horses down there, though, and two men were haying them. More horses than two old nesters would ever need, Canada thought.

Canada studied the place carefully. There was no movement. Nothing to suggest some hardcases were tracking him down. This palisade overlooked the whole country and formed a natural sentry point for that ranch. It was also in the very heart of the rustler country: there were stolen beeves in valleys in every direction. Perhaps the shots hadn't been heard.

As the light dimmed Canada spotted the vague bulk of a single horseman moving downslope to the extreme left. The man was hurrying, but the tumbling trail didn't permit rushing. The dry-gulcher, Canada thought. He eased himself back and walked over to his horses, trying to make sense of what he had seen.

The geldings were restless, stamping unhappily.

He led them downslope into scrub ponderosa and then rubbed each animal down, talking softly. He adjusted the pack on Payday, which had been knocked askew in the high rock.

He had a decision to make, and he did his best deciding when he worked on his horses.

He could head for home now. He had a pretty good idea where the rustled beeves were hiding, and his horses too. This Sanders place was in the middle of it. He could go back to the McFarlands and others, and they could organize a posse or call in some troops.

He was ill-equipped to do more. He had less experience at this sort of manhunting than most any line-riding cowboy of the plains.

Canada frowned and began scraping pebbles and impacted dirt from Crowbait's hooves. The big sorrel nuzzled him in the rump as he bent low and almost butted Canada off his feet. The horse trainer chuckled and rapped the gelding amiably on the jaw.

Fact was, there was an awful lot he still didn't know, he reflected. For instance, he had yet to see the rustlers. He couldn't identify a single one. Nor did he know how many there were, or where they had set guards and bushwack points. A posse could storm in here, see nothing, and get itself all shot up in the process.

Canada eased open the girth and ran his hand up under the blanket, along the sweaty hair of the withers, feeling for soreness or rubbed off hair. Crowbait liked the attention.

"I reckon most of those hardcases are in and out of Grizzly Bear Polarski's," he muttered, not liking the thought that was shaping up in his head. "I could have a look, get to identify a few. Maybe have a few drinks up there," he said to no one in particular.

In truth, Canada was not the man he was an hour earlier, though he didn't know it. The white sunburst of terror has a way of forever changing a man. A terror lived through; a death survived, alters the very nature of his soul.

"There's nothing to lose," he grumbled. "No one to mourn over me if I cash in. I've been alone as long as I can remember. And Linda now. Fat chance that she cares or that a poverty-struck horse trainer would fiddle her tune."

He headed north cautiously in the moonless dark. He reckoned that Roundup was not more than an hour away; from the high palisade he thought he had seen the northern edge of the Bulls and the plains beyond.

Canada was feeling ornery. The ambush still graveled him. He knew he was plumb loco to ride into Polarski's. He picked up a well-beaten trail, probably the main one from Sanders's ranch to Roundup, and he rode it boldly, figuring to bluff in the dark if he were challenged. It was mostly downhill. He passed a lit cabin beside an exposed coal works. A dog yapped, and he hurried on.

He descended at last to the Musselshell, snaking low and shallow. Cottonwoods lined the banks, and beyond cattle grazed the grassy bottoms.

He chose not to ford where the trail intersected the stream. Places like that were sometimes guarded, especially if they came, like this one, into a tough camp from the rear. Off to the west somewhere was the stage road that snaked on up to Grass Range and then to the gold camps around Lewistown. He walked east a few hundred feet and then forded through water barely six inches deep. There were no potholes. He let the horses shake out a moment, and then led Payday into a riverbank thicket and tied him with a slip hitch he could loosen in a hurry. The black would be invisible, even ten yards away.

"Sorry, son, you'll just have to hump there with that pack for a couple of hours," he said softly.

He slid his worn holster off his belt and wrapped the hogleg in the slicker behind the cantle.

"If I can't use a gun like the experts, then I'm safer without one," he muttered. He knew it was true, but he also knew the merciless amusements armed men sometimes enjoyed at the expense of unarmed pilgrims. Rough humor that sometimes perforated a man's soul, and sometimes his toes or limbs. He figured he'd risk it. He was no pilgrim.

He rode a wide loop north past barking hounds, and then angled west until he hit the road. And then south to the saloon squatting on the river.

Polarski's was a long rectangle of heavy logs, hard by the river to the south, and the stage road. There was also a rectangular bunkhouse, a pole corral, and the saloon-keeper's own log home.

The proprietor was a bull of a man, fifty-ish, who poured bad booze, charged high, and kept order with three shotguns under the bar, never more than an arm's reach away. He guzzled more than his clients but showed it less. He was missing an ear that had been shot off, and some fingers that got caught in a baggage-car door. He was devoid of scruple, and even the feisty stage drivers steered clear of the place if they could.

Canada loose-tied Crowbait at the rail, quietly examining the brands on the other mounts. Some were exotic. One horse in particular interested him; it was his own, a young Morgan he had gelded in the fall and had greenbroke. It bore a bar-OB-bar brand, an artistic addition to Canada's CP.

Anger graveled him, but he choked it down, opened the massive plank door, and stepped into a smoky twilight of stale air and unwashed men.

He was in no hurry. He stood a moment, absorbing it all. Kitchen and dining area to the rear. Poker tables and a roulette layout.

A plank bar of rough-sawn jack pine up front. Crowded. Perhaps fifty men, he judged. A small fast-hopping Chinese seemed to manage the kitchen, serve food and drinks, and swamp all at once.

Every manjack in the place wore a gun, some two. There were white pockmarks speckling the walls where lead had collided with wood. Canada had never seen such a collection of artillery. Nor were the side-arms the end of it. Some had shotguns propped beside them. Or rifles. There must have been a dozen Winchester 1873s.

The thought of all those guns popping at each other bemused him. If a man were to bar all the doors from the outside, and then get something started within . . .

"Get in or get out, pilgrim."

The gravel voice was Polarski's. Canada eased up to the bar while the bullet-headed proprietor sloshed a slug of cloudy stuff into a beaker. No choice asked or proffered.

"Two bits coin or gold, no paper."

Canada nodded and paid.

They left him alone then, but didn't ignore him. A bearded gent slipped outside, and then in again, and mumbled things to some tough customers at a rear table. Reading the brand, Canada thought. The CP on Crowbait would tell them much.

The stuff made his eyes water and produced a hiccup or two. They watched him sip it. He watched them watch him. And memorized faces while they did it. The Celestial, barely five feet and developing a belly, scurried glasses and bottles to the tables. The poker games continued desultorily. More than one glance fell upon Canada's bare hip, and then searched his sheepskin coat for a telltale bulge. Polarski kept busy, but his pig eyes never strayed far from the pilgrim. He had a way of glancing, licking his walrus mustache, and turning his back.

Canada felt the gaze of the slim graybearded man down at the far end of the bar; a man who never quite met his own return stare.

"Good evening, Mr. Parker," the gentleman said at last.

Canada was more surprised by the *mister* than by hearing his name.

"You know my brand," Canada replied.

"I believe you're the mustanger over near the 30-Mile."

"Not a mustang on my place."

"Horse breaker, then."

"Never broke a horse in my life. Horse breakers break horses. I train them gentle."

"Well, the Good Lord gives every man a

skill, a trade, and it's up to each of us to do what we can with it, the way we are intended."

Canada was faintly astonished.

"Good broke horses — I mean trained — aren't easy to find out here," the bearded man continued. "Mostly, a drover gets him a mustang, sits him until the vinegar runs out, and steers him with a plow rein. I'm partial to a fine-looking horse myself."

"I saw a nice one at the rail out there," Canada drawled. "A Morgan, looked like. Is that yours?"

"Why, I'm trying him out. Haven't made up my mind yet."

"Who you buyin' him from?" Canada asked softly.

"Oh, I ain't buying. Just trying him out. Grass Range feller raised him," the man replied warily.

"Well, don't buy till you look at mine," Canada grinned. "Some of my stuff is pedigreed, and it's all well trained."

"I'm right partial to blooded horses," the man admitted. "Pedigrees put real value in a beast. You say you've got pedigreed stuff?"

"Some."

"I fancy pedigrees. That's how a man improves the master-work of God."

"And the price tag," Canada muttered.

He didn't like the conversation, and turned a shoulder to stop it.

"I'm Preacher Jonas," the man persisted. "Actually, Jeremiah Jonas, but friends call me Preacher because I've done a heap of it. Built my life on the Good Book, and have it almost memorized." Preacher's gaze darted from Canada's shoulder to his bare hip to his Montana Peak hat with the wide brim.

"You've got a little ventilation up there in the crown, I see," Preacher drawled.

Canada wasn't sure. He hadn't looked. He knew the bullet had plucked his hat. So. Did they have him figured for the intruder up on the palisaded mesa?

"Blackfoot Indian arrow," Canada grinned.

Preacher studied the hole intently for a moment, and then his eyes narrowed. The Chinese, mucking beside the bar, looked up at the hat and frowned. Canada suddenly realized the busy Celestial had been there within earshot for some time.

Well, the hell with it, Canada thought savagely.

"Maybe you can help me, Jonas," he began. "I'm looking for some strayed stock. I thought maybe they drifted this way and I ought to make some inquiries."

"Why, God alone knows what gets into

the skull of a horse," Preacher replied. "They can surely be notional animals. . . . Were the strays pedigreed?"

"Every one," Canada said, suddenly aware he was baiting a hook. It wasn't quite true. The sires were papered, but the dams were carefully selected grade mares, mostly.

"Worth a lot, I suppose," Preacher continued.

"A lot."

"How much, say, on the average?"

"Depends."

"A thousand?"

Canada grinned at the man. "The love of money is the root of all evil," he said slowly.

"Ah! I see you know the Book! Most people confuse that famous verse and think that money itself is the root of all evil. They're wrong, of course. It's the love of it. I confess I sometimes have that lust myself, though I try mightily to stamp it out of my character."

Canada laughed.

The Celestial had bumped his head on the bar while picking up some shattered glass.

"Fat, how does your heathen faith treat money?" Preacher asked amiably.

"As a means to an end," said the little Chinese, slipping off to answer a bellow from a poker table.

"This country's full of those heathen," Preacher said. "Opium eaters mostly. Not fit company."

Canada found himself amused. He turned to find Polarski staring at him. The glass had been refilled.

"I didn't order it," he said mildly.

"I say you did," growled Polarski.

Canada reached into his dungarees and dropped the double eagle on the counter. This was no place to argue the niceties.

Preacher's eyes darted to the gold, then away, while Polarski made change and the Chinaman unloaded glasses.

"Tell me more about pedigrees," Preacher probed casually.

"I can't rightly remember them all," Canada replied. "All those Jockey Club papers are back in my cabin. The black stud, now, he's pure race-bred, right from Eclipse. Funny, he's one of the ones that took off."

"What all are you missing?"

"Oh, that Thoroughbred. Some Morgans. A quarter stud. Some good mares, and a lot of young stuff."

"Some ornery horse thief may have got them," Preacher said earnestly. "Stock like that, you know the temptation. There's always some with the devil in 'em. You know how the prayer goes: Lead us not into temptation. Well, they sure get tempted." He shook his head sadly. "It's getting so a man can hardly hang on to his stock, the bad hombres are so thick. But, praise the Lord, old Granville Stuart's organizing a protective association up at Gilt Edge to shake out the noose and put the hemp to work. I've been thinking of joinin', but I can't. I'm just a small operator. Say, now, how many of those blooded horses, those registered beasts, are you still raising?"

"Oh, maybe a hundred," said Canada, multiplying horses like the loaves and fishes.

The eyes of the gray-bearded gentleman flared open.

"I don't see how you can handle 'em all alone."

"Most of them I don't. Just raise 'em and sell 'em off. But the ones I handle I charge plenty for, and they're worth it. . . . They're most all for sale." Canada shifted. "Time for me to mosey on home, Mr. Jonas. I might offer a little reward for those strays. Spread the word around, will you?"

Canada drained his glass and slid away from the bar, colliding with the Celestial. A glass flew and shattered.

"That comes off your wage, Fat," Polarski roared. "Now clean it up pronto."

"A thousand pardons," said the small man, peering up at Canada. "Vessels are broken in the night. We must avoid collisions."

Canada slammed the heavy door and stood quietly a moment, absorbing the hush of the night. Sagebrush scented the air. He was unharmed. On the trail he could mull over what he had learned, sort out his impressions. That Preacher, now, with all that eye-rolling piety — who was *he*?

There was no one in sight. Canada slipped aboard Crowbait, slid a hand under the slicker to make sure the old hogleg was there, and trotted the impatient gelding toward the river. He picked up Payday and returned to the stage road — no sense pushing over tough hill trails all night — to go south to the VP. A night breeze made the cottonwoods hiss, and a coyote barked maliciously beyond some misty hill.

The bantam man with the pointy black beard, known as Yuma here but once known as Brevet Major Jereboam Harkness, slid quietly to the side of Preacher Jonas and then stepped quietly into the night, only moments after Canada had taken his leave. Yuma was smiling.

Several men who knew that smile watched

him leave and winked at each other. The poker players returned to their cards, the night's diversion over.

Yuma repaired to his private quarters, a board-and-batt house north of Polarski's, and there opened a long box of polished cherry and withdrew from its silk-lined interior a weapon of extraordinary precision crafted in London by Caulkins and Woolcott. He slipped twelve shiny brass cartridges into the repeater's magazine and then walked swiftly to his lineback dun, a horse of neutral color, carefully chosen for its invisibility, surefootedness, and bottom. Carrying the lightweight Yuma, the horse could go twenty-four hours at fast-paces, trotting, loping, galloping if it had to, and still have reserve.

He set off, then, ten minutes behind Canada, his thin lips compressed the way they usually were when he was going to do someone a favor. An hour later he was lying in a natural rock fortress at the top of a long grade where a slow-moving traveler would pass within fifty yards of his gunsights. There was a new moon; little but starlight. A hard shot in the murk, but an easy escape if things went wrong. He saw the bulks of two horses and one rider laboring slowly upgrade, and his lips distended.

Canada felt something slam wickedly into his chest before he heard a report. Then something slammed along his head, and the stars disappeared from the black sky, and he felt himself falling.

Yuma ejected the shiny cartridges, half again as long as most, and slid the rifle into its scabbard, feeling a little lightheaded. He stepped delicately down the hill, stared at the body — the head was a mass of blood and the chest was black with it — and caught the packhorse. The other, the sorrel, circled warily away, frustrating Yuma's hope of catching the reins. He shrugged. The packhorse would yield more anyway. He led it back to his dun, and trotted toward Roundup.

He felt giddy. He always felt giddy, especially when he had favored a tall one like Parker or those big wide ones down at the territorial prison.

He cut east into the hills toward Pike and Maudie's. When he did a favor, he never liked to hang around a place where he might be seen.

CHAPTER SEVEN

A physician knelt beside the sprawled hulk of Canada Parker, examining him by the light of an acetylene torch.

"He's alive, though he probably won't make it," the short doctor said to the man beside him, a coal miner from the pits at Klein. "I'm a bit rusty; haven't practiced for ten years," he added, listening carefully to the irregular heartbeat and the gurgling chest wound below the right shoulder.

The rotund doctor worked swiftly. "Right lung's full of blood. Head wound is not so bad, except for a concussion. Superficial bleeding. That punctured lung is what I'm worried about."

After twenty minutes of fast work, Canada Parker's wounds were bound; blood loss stopped; throat cleared of tissue and fluids; head wrapped, and pulse steadied into a weak flutter. They lifted him into the waiting buckboard and wrapped him warmly.

"Hanging by a thread. He isn't likely to make it to 30-Mile," the doctor said grimly. "I tried to warn him, but he missed it. Let's wait a few minutes and see how he does. Then I must get back."

"Where'd you learn medicine?" asked the miner.

"Harvard, class of '67," the doctor replied. "I also have degrees in botany, engineering, and Oriental studies."

"But you gave it all up to come run our Denver office," the miner grinned.

"I gave up nothing, really," the doctor retorted. "I've used every one of my disciplines, and more, with the agency. In fact, Pinkerton's turned out to be the perfect occupation for my various humble skills and interests."

"Can't argue with you a-tall. You've broken more cases than the rest of us put together," the miner said.

The doctor drew himself up. "Time to go. I can't be missing long. They serve flapjacks beginning at seven, or rather, I do, even though I have to swamp the place after they close at midnight. It's wearing me down . . ."

"Drive's going to take a while," the miner sighed.

"Go slowly. Check Parker regularly. Don't reveal yourself to the McFarlands. Get word to Bell if you can, if you should meet the stage."

The doctor mounted his small horse and trotted north; the miner rumbled south with his unconscious cargo.

Three hours later he banged on the door at the 30-Mile, shivering in the predawn cold. He heard some signs of life at last, and finally the door of the veranda opened and Stuart McFarland peered out, kerosene lamp in one hand, shotgun in the other.

"I've brought Canada Parker to you. He's been shot and needs care. Very near dead," the miner said apologetically.

McFarland stared at the stranger, then at the reclining bulk in the wagon.

"For God's sake, man, bring him in!" he roared, just as Anne appeared in her robe.

The burly stranger lifted Canada as if he were a lamb, and followed the McFarlands to the bedroom where Anne silently beckoned him.

Canada was gray in the lamplight, and the gurgle of each irregular breath terrified Anne. She tucked him in with question marks upon her face.

"We don't know who did it," the miner said, looking from father to daughter.

"I'll kill the sonofabitch," Stuart muttered.

"You'll have to wait in line," Anne said

tartly. "Who's *we*? Who are you?"

"I mine coal up yonder. Name's Robards. I got him to a doc. Here's some powders for him if his pulse becomes ragged. You're to force plenty of warm liquids into him if he lives."

"How'd you know to come here?" Stuart demanded.

"I can't say," the miner said quietly. "But I'd like you to convey this news to Thomas Bell, of the NP, on the next stage south."

"He's a friend, and we'll do it. If you're tied to Tom Bell in any way, why just count on us for anything needin'."

"Parker's horse followed me all the way down and is in the yard."

"Crowbait!" Anne cried. "We'll catch him, if we can."

"There's no doc in Roundup," grumbled McFarland. "Whole thing doesn't make a blamed bit of sense. I've more questions than a sow has tits."

Robards smiled thinly. "Let them lie. Just take care of him. He's a good man."

"He's more than a good man!" Anne shot back at him. "There's not another like him with horses. I wish he had the same way with — oh, never mind. Canada, goddam you skinny independent mule-headed smart-mouthed stinking blue-nosed jackass,

126

you *live* or I'll know the reason why," she bellowed, crying, twisting his leaden hand in her own moist one.

The men clumped down the stairs to catch up Crowbait, while Anne sat on the bed and wept and scolded.

"It was those rustlers, I know it. I knew you'd get in too close, you goddam mule. Got hit in your thick head, too, damn you. Look at you, all caked with dirt and blood. I'll have to wash you up. You'll have to forgive me, you ornery old hermit, but I'm going to have to yank off your boots and pants."

Two hours later she fell into a fitful sleep in the rocker beside him, listening to his gurgling breath come in frightful spasms.

She kissed him, just as she had done every day. But this time it awakened him from the long coma. He stared at her.

"You kissed me," he whispered.

She was startled.

"You're damn right I did," she replied. "I figured it was the only chance I'd ever get."

He closed his eyes. Listening drained his energies.

"And besides," she added, "I know I'll never tie knots with you even if I wanted."

He stared up at her again, at the rings of

rich brown hair tumbling over her shoulders. Liquid brown eyes and creamy skin. The top of her shirtwaist was unbuttoned and the beige cotton swelled tightly over her full figure.

"Good conformation," he mumbled. "For using, not for racing."

She smiled. "Why don't you ask me how long you've laid flat in that bed?"

"Don't want to know," he said.

"Well I'll tell you. Seventeen days."

"Not long enough," he muttered.

"Why don't you ask me who took care of you? Fed you and bathed you?"

"I've no secrets left," he grumbled.

"Not a one," she snapped.

"How did I get here?"

"We don't know the sum of it," she said softly. "You were brought in by a miner we'd never met. You'd been doctored."

"Doctored?"

"Wounds dressed, some heart powders, and all."

"No doctor in the Bulls," he grumbled.

"Then a passing angel saved your bacon."

"Kiss me again," he demanded.

"Like hell I will. Not when you're awake," she sputtered. "Save it for your widow friend."

"I suppose I talked about her the whole

time," he said.

"No, you never even mentioned her name."

"Then —"

"I can read your skinny four-legged mind, and don't you forget it. As for this" — she waved her hand at the sickroom — "it's my duty." She laughed wickedly.

"Who shot me?"

"I was going to ask you the same question."

"I don't hurt."

"You would if you tried to move."

"Where's Crowbait?"

"Out in the corral, eating his heart out for you."

Canada smiled sweetly, and slept.

"Canada, can you talk a little?"

He opened his eyes and stared up at Stuart McFarland and the other man, whom he remembered as Bell, from Billings.

"I'll try. You want any information I can give."

"How are you feeling? You had a close shave," Bell said quietly. "You're lucky."

"I'll manage," Canada said. But pain stabbed his chest and he coughed. "Most every locked-in valley north of the VP has rustled cattle. Darn few don't. The traveled ones don't," he said. "Every brand in central Montana. Saw plenty of VPs. That rundown Sanders outfit seemed to be the center of it, near as I could tell. It's guarded, but I don't know by who, or how many. I don't know who's the head man either, but I have some notions. I looked a few over at Grizzly Bear's."

"The night you were shot?" asked Bell.

"Don't remember," Canada said. "I just can't remember anything."

"We'll go in and clean 'em out," snapped McFarland. "I've strung up a few in my day."

"Don't!" Canada said wearily. "You'll lose men."

"We'll go, dammit, and make them taste some lead."

"Like George Custer," Canada whispered.

Stuart McFarland wanted his cattle back. He was missing over seven hundred, near as he and his crew could tally, mostly mother cows. He'd hardly seen his own spring calf crop.

One May day he resolved to go up into the hills after them. If they were there, he'd get 'em out. He had five or six good men, men who had sand and had seen both ends of a gun before. Not the least among these was his foreman, Fireball Fenton. The fellow was potbellied, bullnecked, gap-toothed, bandy-legged, and on the shady side of fifty, but he had done some hard fighting in his day against Indians, Rebs, and bandits.

Canada had warned him he'd be biting off a plug he couldn't chew, but that horse trainer was no fighter, Stuart figured. He wouldn't know how easily an armed outfit, with some tough hombres, could collect those beeves and maybe string a little rope over a cottonwood limb for the fun of it.

He put together his company and rode first to Canada's little spread, quiet in the morning sun.

"I'll check the cabin," said Fireball, easing off the big dun.

Stuart nodded.

"It's all tore up," Fireball announced, blinking in the sunlight a moment later. "Like someone was looking for something."

"Wonder what they thought Canada had in there — gold?" Stuart ruminated. "Almighty odd, but probably not connected with the rustling."

They trailed north to the VP, ten miles farther into the Bulls.

"Ride careful, gents," McFarland cautioned. "Keep your eyes open; search the rims. If we're shot at, don't bunch up like ducks."

He cast a worried glance backward. Five tough hands in addition to himself; two spare mounts, and two packhorses. He surveyed the loads on the packhorses; they were balanced and low, the way they should be to keep a horse from getting sored up.

"I should have sent a man — Clancy maybe — up there to the VP to watch over things after Canada caught it. Sorry I didn't," Stuart said privately to Fireball.

"They ain't likely to be one critter on the place," Fireball said. "Them cows'll be scarce as mosquitoes in December."

He was wrong. The bulls that had been recovered at Pompeys Pillar dotted the pastures as they approached the somnolent ranch buildings.

"Whoa up . . . let's just study this a minute, so we don't get our tails shot off," Stuart said uneasily. They saw nothing. No glint of steel or open windows.

"Clancy — you and Ramirez ride around south and come in that away. Bulldog, you and Murchison go around the opposite, come down the slope. Fireball and I'll just go in on the road."

They did, and sprung their trap upon no one. Nothing. The drovers collected in the silent yard, staring uneasily at the rims.

"Not a horse in sight. I thought Canada had his whole remuda over here," Fireball said. "Those horses of his stuck closer to him than spring ticks on a heifer."

"There's no horses, for sure. I think they cleaned the horses out, at least, even if they figgered the Hereford bulls were too hot to touch," Stuart agreed. "Well, we'll have to tell the patient he's lost the rest. It ain't gonna help his healing any."

"Place is spooky," said Clancy. "I've got me the feeling there's eyes upon me, but blamed if I see anyone."

"So do I," said Fireball. It was an intuition that had kept him alive in his Indian-fighting days.

They stayed the night in the comfortable bunkhouse and trailed out soon after dawn.

"Today we'll get in the thick of it, soon as we cut loose of the VP," Stuart predicted.

He detailed riders to check adjacent valleys and look over the country from nearby ridges. They all returned with a shake of the head. The Bull Mountains were empty.

They pushed north beyond VP range and never saw a cow. McFarland detailed riders far to the east and west, checking every locked-in valley, sighting from each ridge, pushing through grassy parks and pine glades. Nothing.

"Damned if I know where the critters are hid. Canada said each valley's full of 'em," Stuart muttered.

"I think they were, but ain't now," Clancy volunteered. "Those cowpies, now. Some are pretty fresh. Not all dried out and gray, like they get when they're older than sam hill. Still brown. Not new and green, but soft and brown."

"That means the beeves were in here and are being pushed out of sight for our benefit," Fireball deduced. "Pretty slick, but it sure worries me some."

"Least they ain't shooting at us," Stuart said. "God knows, that cap rock and sandstone and all the jack pine is cover enough to stand off an army."

"Figger it this way," Fireball persisted. "By hiding those beeves, they're sayin' they're here. Canada's right. They're here, thick as warts on a toad. And we may be walkin' into something."

"Don't look like we'll get much 30-Mile stock," Stuart grumbled. "We better damn well git some of it back or there may be no more 30-Mile Ranch much longer. If we pick up other brands, we'll bring 'em out too. And sort later."

They pushed deeper, through country

unknown to them all. Everywhere there was tantalizing sign, but never a beeve. Fresh-cloven hoofprints. An occasional stamp of a shod horse. Grass recently cropped. Some salt at a spring.

"We're being watched," Fireball said itchily. "Better post guards tonight. I'm gittin' more and more restless, the way I used to. When the rheumatiz flares up, I know they're comin'."

Nothing happened. The next day was cloudy and the drovers were tired from lack of sleep.

"I think I see a beeve over yonder," Clancy said, about mid-morning.

"Get him and bring him in. I want to look at that brand," Stuart snapped. Weariness and frustration flushed his face.

The lanky redhead trotted off while they waited in a locked-up flat. They watched him trot up a coulee, disappear into a pine grove, and emerge on top, under a leaden sky. The critter was there, all right, and skittered over the slope and out of sight. Clancy built his loop, went after her, topping the ridge, and disappeared.

It was the last they ever saw of him.

They waited an hour. Then they rode up the slope, supposing perhaps that he had fallen and was hurt. They found his tracks, and the beeve's leading into cap rock. Where they disappeared altogether. They called. They fired their pistols. They spent the rest of the leaden day hunting the missing drover in every thicket for a mile around. But he was gone, vanished like a ghost.

They made an uneasy camp, this time in a defensible park in the rims. Each man stuck to himself that night, and more than one cleaned his pistol or carbine.

Stuart sank into a beefy silence, so thick that even Fireball, a twenty-year companion, left him alone, crabbing at the universe.

Fireball had seen the Indians do it. One man at a time, never visible, always present. Fear crawled up in his big gut and stayed coiled there.

"Okay, you'll think I'm six kinds of dude," Murchison said suddenly, breaking the terrible silence. "But I think a man should get a send-off when he dies."

He looked at the rest, and they averted their eyes.

"Well, I'm a-going to do it," he said bitterly.

And he did. "Our Father," he said, in a soft tenor that rolled into the starless sky. The others listened silently, secretly pleased. It was the death the cowboys feared most — the unknown kind, somewhere lonesome, with no one standing by. If, of course, Clancy was dead. But they all knew he was, somewhere, with a pile of rock on top.

They worked methodically the next day, but stayed banded together for safety. They zigzagged generally northward, never finding beeves, but constantly tripping over sign. Some defined trails showed up now, leading to the northeast, to a large flat, perhaps a square mile or so, they could see from the ridges. They rode there, warily.

On the west side of the flat some forlorn ranch buildings huddled miserably, surrounded by tumbledown fence, collapsed pole corrals, and unnameable debris.

"It must be the Sanders lash-up," McFarland said. "I never did see it."

"Lookit this here grass," Fireball exclaimed. "All eaten down and stamped just when it should be pushing up."

"It's been used hard," Stuart agreed. "Lots of sagebrush in it, going to hell like this whole outfit."

They paused a good rifle shot from the place.

"Look. If this is the hangout of these hardcases, we'd be fools to wander in there," Fireball cautioned.

"I'm going in alone, neighborlike," Stuart said.

"But — !"

"But nothing. I'm gonna do it."

In fact, the probable death of Clancy was clawing at Stuart's heart. Fireball knew it and disagreed, even though he knew what was goading the boss.

The rancher rode easily but observed sharply from the shade of his high-crowned hat. There was filth; the smell of the outhouse caught him in the yard. The one thing that seemed halfway fixed was the sodroof bunkhouse.

Pike Sanders emerged from somewhere, and Stuart absorbed the man's decay as he rode up.

"You're Mr. Sanders, I presume. I'm Stuart McFarland, your neighbor down at 30-Mile."

Pike yawned unhappily. "What's yer business?" he said at last.

"Checking strays, sir. Mind if I have a look at your stock? I haven't seen any, but your spring grass here's been used hard."

"I ain't got any beef. I just lease the grass to some others."

"Oh? Who's that, may I ask?"

"Well it ain't yer business — what's this, some inquisition?"

"Are they here?"

"They come and go. None here now that

I know of."

"What brands?"

"I don't know. I never had a look."

Stuart believed him. The man looked as though he rarely got a hundred yards from his house.

"Mind if I look around?"

Sanders shrugged his shoulders and turned to go inside.

"Well, thanks for the hospitality," Stuart said wryly. He rode slowly to the bunkhouse and kicked open the door. It was in use. Clothing and tack strewn about. Tobacco scent heavy in the air. He backed out and boarded his stringy horse.

The palisades caught his eye. All along the west flank of the flat they rose, the final heights of a majestic mesa that commanded the whole country.

The mesa intrigued him. He couldn't put a finger on any reason, but he almost smelled cattle that direction, almost heard them bawling, too. The decision came fast, and without his usual caution.

"We're going to top that mesa," he announced to his waiting crew. "I've got a feeling we'll learn something up there. Sanders was no help at all, but this is the place, all right. We're in the middle."

They rode through the ranch, hit a westward trail that curled upslope upon the broad shoulder of the mesa, entered a defile that rose more steeply, encountered ponderosas and junipers along the trail, and emerged into an area of jagged sandstone blocks, cracked vertically like slices of cheese, and strewn loosely on the slopes rising above.

"I declare I can hear cattle up there," he cried pushing ahead.

"I don't like it a-tall, Stuart," Fireball cautioned. "Let's take stock here a moment."

The shots came in a volley. Murchison sunk down wordlessly, a bullet through his mouth. Ramirez tumbled over sideways, his body flipping and twisting on the ground as the life ran out. A slug whipped past Fireball's ear; he wheeled his horse into the cover of slabrock. Stuart's horse went out from under him. The rancher fell, and a shot slashed his arm as he hit the earth. He crabbed toward Fireball and the shelter there. Bulldog died from a slug through his heart as he was wheeling around to get away.

Fireball wasted no time. He grabbed his old friend, heaved him up on a wandering horse, yanked his own dun to safety, and scrambled sideways into the juniper, out of the coulee of death, while lead whipped the trees. He didn't stop for an hour. Then he wrapped McFarland's arm and led the pale rancher's half-crazed horse south.

It was the longest two-day ride they had ever known.

Chapter Eight

Grief hung thick over the 30-Mile. Stuart McFarland retreated into silence and rarely emerged from his bedroom, where he sat for hours on end before a tintype of his darkly pretty wife, who had died seven years before.

Fireball Fenton kept things going, piling harsh labor on the seven once-carefree cowboys who still remained at the haunted ranch. Sidearms flowered, and the evenings were full of the staccato rattle of practice shooting.

Anne staggered on, trying to hold her shaky household together. At night in bed she wept for them all, but especially for Clinton Clancy, the genial redheaded Texan whom she half loved and always had bantered with.

Canada hobbled silently about for the hour or two each day he could stand without feeling faint. He healed amid an almost mortuary gloom that black-curtained life around him. Each day he walked slowly down to the corrals and spent time with Crowbait, and only then did his old joy sneak back. In the McFarland house his heart was leaden.

He was sorry for them all, sorry that Stuart hadn't heeded his warning. He could say nothing; the bull-headed rancher had drunk bitterly the juices of recklessness.

One day Canada tried to ride Crowbait, but the effort failed. He couldn't lift the saddle up, and the chest wound shot back pain when he tried. But he was healing nonetheless, and each day he was able to lift his high-cantled saddle a little higher.

Reports filtered in from the stage drivers and teamsters hauling coal south. There had been more deaths and disappearances. Some of Ezekiel Earley's crew had been dry-gulched. A sheriff's deputy had died from ambush. An unknown man had disappeared.

"Leastwise, no one's touched the stages," one driver told Canada. "But even with an extra man riding shotgun, I'm powerful glad when we get shut of those hills."

Rumor had it that a large cattle drive had left the Bulls for Deadwood, South Dakota, and that there had been hundreds of Herefords sighted among the longhorns. But no one knew for sure, and the country was too thinly populated to track down a story like that.

Canada began riding each day, at first for an hour and then two. He wondered if he'd ever get his strength back. Some men didn't, he knew. They were permanently shattered. Just beyond the trails he chose lay the first outriders of the Bulls, rising up, reef upon reef, out of the northern prairies. His horses were there — somewhere. The ranch he was pledged to care for was there — untended. And yet the pay still came from Bell for the work he couldn't do at a ranch where death lurked.

He grew restless. The eerie silence hadn't lifted at the 30-Mile. Stuart said little and slouched in a rocker on the veranda. The loss of a third of his cattle no longer aroused him; the possible loss of the rest was something only Fireball fussed about. Time didn't heal a thing, though the ranch cried out, like an animal, for release from its torture.

Canada had a hankering to see his own ranch. Surely, he thought, it wouldn't be guarded the way the VP might be. He was strong enough now. It wasn't all that far from the 30-Mile, and he could slip into it from the west, the trackless side of the Bulls.

He told no one at the silent McFarland home. They were used to his comings and goings as he healed. He saddled Crowbait before dusk, when the full June moon was swimming over the hills, and he set off west, in the hush of twilight when all the world was stilled. A mile from the 30-Mile headquarters he cut north up a long swale and then worked east in higher and rougher country that he guessed was some of his rearmost land, where he didn't often come.

The worry left him; the night was too friendly for it and the crickets too pleasant in the rare Montana heat. He spotted a stone-crowned hill he knew, lordly above his main hay meadow, and soon looked down on his own fields where high grass begged for the mower and rake. It grieved him to see good hay go ungathered.

He stood a moment looking down upon his own land in the moonlight, and loving his place.

"There's no room for a woman on it," he said sternly, beating back the thought that lay upon him heavily that night.

He was in no hurry. He dismounted, letting Crowbait crop the spring grass while he watched and waited. There was no movement. He knew there wouldn't be in this

obscure corner. After a while he led Crowbait into his ranch yard and tied him in
shadow. The white light flooding into his
cabin revealed a chaotic mess. What he had
left behind had been scattered. Pack rats
had nested in his tick.

He had left the Jockey Club papers in a
tin box, which now lay upon the floor, bereft
of its contents.

"Gotcha," grinned Canada sourly, thinking of the gentle probing of that pious fraud
at Grizzly Bear's.

He was weary. It was a demoralizing thing
to see all he had built laid waste. Not a
horse in sight. His chest hurt. He rode to
the McFarlands' the way he came and
unsaddled Crowbait around midnight when
the moon was a hard white ball.

He stepped quietly onto the veranda.

"What did you find there?" Anne's voice
rose out of the shadows.

"What?"

"I told you I can read your mind, Canada
Parker. You went up to your spread like a
damn fool."

He sighed. "I found that the man I talked
to the night I got shot stole my horses.
Every damn one 'cept Crowbait."

She was silent.

"I don't think it'll ever change or be the

same," she sighed. "Dad will never be the same. He died inside when he and Fireball came back alone. Plumb died. So did I, I guess. I don't know what I'll do. I just exist. I'd have chosen you if you had asked. I could have given — oh hell, I'm sorry I said it."

"I'm sorry you said it, too," Canada replied sharply.

She stormed inside.

He sulked on the veranda for an hour.

At breakfast he told the McFarlands he was going back to the VP. He was braced for a storm of objections but got none. He was uneasy. He had intended to get mad, but now he was deprived of the chance. Worse, his fondness for these dearest friends, and his gratitude for weeks of loving care, all conspired to tie his tongue.

"I'm going to send Fireball with you for a while," Stuart said softly. "It's time I got to running the 30-Mile again."

"What are you going to do there?" Anne asked Canada sadly.

"Why — hold it for the Van Pelts." The question bothered him. In fact he was going there to get away from the 30-Mile and its gloom.

They left at ten, about when the late June sun was bedding down. At five, with the first gray streaking the east, they slipped into the silent VP yard. They had been cautious but had met no trouble, traveling a wide loop from known roads. Canada was exhausted and slept into the afternoon. Fireball restlessly stalked the slopes commanding the ranch, studying every cranny until he was satisfied that he knew where spies and bushwackers might lurk. The place was vulnerable. A sharpshooter could cover the front door, the yard, the well, and all but a few corners sheltered by the barn. The well in particular was a danger. Anyone pumping it would be an immobilized target, and its creaking would deafen anyone to danger. Fireball didn't like the lash-up at all. He was a fighting man, not a sitting duck. If Parker wanted to stay here like a bull's-eye, that was his business. But any durned fool would know that the hills themselves were safer.

He said so at supper.

"This here is a deathtrap," he began. "If'n you want another hole through you, why just sit here and wait for it because she's a-coming. We'd do better just roaming these hills, looking for beeves, maybe rustlin' away from the rustlers."

"I haven't the strength yet," Canada replied. "You go ahead; there's no need for you to nursemaid me. That's what Stuart really had in mind, but it's not necessary."

"Those are my instructions," Fireball said flatly. "Stick tighter than a burr in the tail."

Canada didn't argue. "Well, let's do what we can to prepare for emergencies until I'm stronger on my pins," he said.

That suited Fireball. The next day they drew emergency water and stored it in the kitchen. Canada put Crowbait in a half-roofed corral beside the barn. They checked the thick shutters on the house, once used for protection against Indians. They readied gear for a quick getaway.

"I never did hear tell what you found out at Grizzly's the night you were shot," Fireball said.

"The place was crowded, but there were one or two caught my eye, and one I talked to some," Canada recollected. "He was a thin gray-bearded man, maybe forty, called himself Preacher Jonas. And he sounded like one, too, always quoting the Bible."

"I know the one," Fenton said softly. "Probably the most dangerous man on the frontier. You know why? It's not because he's pretending to be a good man, when he ain't. He's no hypocrite. But because everything he learned about good character makes him a stronger man than the rest of those owlhoots.

"He's taken all the things go into a decent man and harnessed 'em to his greed, knowin' he's doing it but still maybe believing in the good. He's no drunk; rarely loses his temper. No womanizer. Doesn't smoke. He controls others by sort of reminding them of their weakness. I think he's the son of some sort of revivalist and still hankers for all them things those people promise. But you know, try as he might, he just can't look another man in the eye."

"That's the one," said Canada. "He's a horse thief."

"It'd be easy for him to get some hardcases together," Fireball continued. "That gospel business, funny the effect it has on outlaws. Some are starving for it; they's not many men who figure they're plumb bad. Others of 'em regard this Preacher as an odd duck, but they follow along, because he's got no vices and has some ability to command. Truth is, he can endure more trouble than most; suffer more, take command easier. He's a ruthless one. If'n he's in these Bulls buildin' a fortress, then we've got big trouble."

"He's the one," sighed Canada. "But I don't know for sure he's the ringleader."

"I met him years ago at some Kansas railheads, after driving up beef from Texas. I've kept track. Stagecoach drivers going through here, they're always full of news."

"What's he likely to do here?" Canada asked.

Fireball mulled it over for a moment.

"Two things are plain enough. He won't be likin' the company he keeps — he hankers to go respectable, as if it were some kind of suit he could put on. I'd wager he'll clean out the hardcases soon as he can. And the other thing is, he'll try to buy the VP. It suits him, now that I think of it. He would kill and swindle and terrorize just so he can make himself an empire builder here. I never did see such a man . . ."

"I've been wondering who shot me. He was there that night."

"Preacher could do it, but he's a pistol man, not a bushwacker. I doubt that he pulled that trigger."

"I do too, somehow. I don't know what I'd do if I ever found the one. I've never killed anyone in my life, and don't intend to if I can help it," Canada said. "But I might get a little riled up."

"Sonny, you'd better not try. Leave it to the sandy ones and stick to your horse trainin'."

"I don't happen to have any horses to

train," Canada snapped.

"You may never get 'em back," Fireball warned. "You're up against a one who's tough and smart and meaner than any ten Canadas."

Canada grinned.

"What's gonna happen to this place. Are the Van Pelts goin' to sell it?" Fireball asked.

"They'll sell, I reckon," Canada sighed. "Linda — the widow — she won't be back. It was a busted dream for her."

"I've seen busted dreams often enough," Fireball said.

The faint sound of bawling cattle drifted through the open windows.

"Something's bothering those bulls," Canada said, looking.

"It don't sound like no bulls," Fireball replied, heading for the window. "Now what in sam hill is that?"

Cresting the eastern meadows, heavy in the dust, was a mass of cattle, uniformly brown and white.

"Herefords, couple hundred of 'em lest my eyeballs be lying to me," Fireball announced.

"And some drovers too, but I don't figure how many in that dust."

The cows spread out gradually in the bull pasture until the whole southern meadows were a mass of bellowing cattle.

"Lookit those bulls. They ain't seen a cow in months!" Fireball laughed.

"That's it. They drove those cows back here for breeding. They needed those bulls that were brought back here."

"Let's get out of here!" Fireball snapped. "There's four or five hardcases out there, maybe more coming."

"There's just cows and calves in that bunch."

"Come on, dammit," Fireball roared, "while we can!"

They raced out to the barn and saddled fast. Their duffel was ready. They loaded it on as they watched five riders emerge from the dust and ride easily toward the ranch buildings.

"Follow me," Fireball growled.

They trotted through shadows, curled behind the barns, and slipped into the jack pines to the east.

"If we're spotted we're dead ducks," Fireball whispered. "You're no fighter, you're wounded, and I don't like the odds." In fact he was glad to escape rather than try to defend the log house with a man and a half. He could hear the bawling of the cattle down below, and was glad of the noise.

"That graybeard down there, that's Jonas,

ain't it?" Fireball asked.

"Yes. And that's the pointy-bearded bantam that's his sidekick. I saw him at Grizzly's too. Looks like they're expecting trouble, the way they've got their carbines out."

Preacher rode carefully around the log house and reined up to peer into a window. It didn't take him long to discover that someone had made a hasty exit. He ordered his hardcases to search the yard, revolvers drawn. They found green manure in the corrals, but no horses or humans.

From their shadowed thicket on the eastern ridge, Canada and Fireball watched Jonas emerge from the log house and carefully study the surrounding hills. The hardcases returned, then, and he led them off to the north, guns drawn, and all of them ready for action.

"He's usin' the place like he owned it. But he's takin' no chances. That bunch won't touch this place till it's bought, I'll reckon. He wants it so bad I could feel it plumb up here atop this rock," Fireball muttered.

"They'll be watching it," Canada warned. "Every day, from now on. Some one of those buzzards will check on those Herefords and the waters, and have a look-see at the headquarters. Maybe it'll be that

Preacher himself, long as he wants this lash-up so bad."

They waited an hour or so, until they were sure none of the hardcases had doubled back.

"Let's go down and have a look at those cows and calves," Fireball said. "We might learn somethin'."

They rode quietly down the slopes until they reached the broad southern flats. None of the cow brands had been altered as far as they could see. But the Hereford calves each carried a new brand, still healing in most cases: the XX.

"I guess they figure those VP Herefords are too hot to handle or alter," Canada said. "We may as well stay at the log house tonight. We'll be spotted here for certain within a few days, but tonight seems safe enough."

Fireball nodded. They put the geldings back in the sheltered pens and arranged their gear for a fast exit again. The big log house seemed cold, even hostile, and neither of them was happy to be there, despite its comforts.

"We'd likely be trapped here if they found us out. I don't know what I can accomplish here anyway," Canada said.

"I'm glad the light has glimmered up

inside your horse-trainer skull," Fireball said malevolently.

"Trouble is, I'm weak as a pup, and outdoor livin' wears a man down fast. Healthy ones almost as much as ones in my shape. Food's bad, sleep's worse, the dirt is unhealthy, and the labor's three times what it is in quarters. But I guess I'll have to do it. We need a lot more facts. That Preacher now. He looked like the ramrod down there, but we don't know it. There could be someone above him. We don't know who's doing the dry-gulching."

Canada sighed. "It looks like that Preacher is just going to settle in and raise Herefords up here. He can't sell any, not for a long time, after Pompeys Pillar. First buyer or stationmaster he'd talk to would finger him. So it looks like he'll just multiply those brown-and-white-face critters while he rustles the longhorns from spreads like the 30-Mile and peddles them. Soon as he buys the VP and has a bill of sale, it's all up and up for him to sell those Herefords."

"So you got theories, but nothing to peg 'em to," Fireball concluded. "Course, that wouldn't stop a necktie party no how. Sometimes it's better to string 'em first and ask all them polite questions later!"

The next morning it rained. A thunderstorm built up in the night and tore loose at dawn. By nine it was hailing, but an hour later it settled into a light drizzle.

"Hell of a day to abandon the comforts of home," Fireball grumbled. "But I'd rather get wet than shot."

They loaded the gear into panniers and then onto Fireball's dun. Another load was anchored behind Canada's saddle on Crowbait. With only two horses, and Canada needing to ride, they would have to make two trips up to a cave that Canada knew of, where they could camp.

Wearing their yellow slickers, they headed north, with Fireball unhappily leading his dun. The rain dripped down their necks and into their boots. They arrived about the time the clouds were breaking. The cave was dry but cold, and well concealed by a slab of sandstone in front of the mouth.

"How'd you find this?" Fireball asked, obviously pleased.

"Looking for VP cattle. Pure accident," Canada grinned. "There's another place I'll show you, a niche sort of hollowed out of cap rock. I took Mrs. Van Pelt there once."

They unloaded, dragged some deadwood into the opening to dry, and then set off for the VP once again.

"That yeller slicker's too much of an

advertisement, Canada," Fireball warned. Canada rolled it and tied it behind the cantle. "Sun's out so we'll have to be watchful."

They stared down upon the soggy ranch from the west ridge and saw nothing. It was somnolent in the moist afternoon. They went in then, both palpably afraid of the possibility of ambush. This trip was mostly for foodstuffs. They loaded flour and beans and bacon into the panniers; a bag of oats for the horses; and a sack of coffee, salt, and sugar for Canada to carry on his lap.

They eased out of the big house just as the glint of metal flashed from the eastern ridge. There was a high bark — some sort of bullet Fireball had never heard before, but one that sent terror through Canada — and the whip of lead into the doorframe.

"I'm climbin' behind you," Fireball snapped. He yanked the oats off, and bounded onto Crowbait's massive rump.

"Move!" he barked. A screeching bullet clipped the dun's packsaddle.

Canada ditched the duffel he was holding, and kicked the gelding. He and the burly Fireball were too much, even for Crowbait. The foreman still had the dun's lead rope in hand and together they careened westward, a naked target for the bushwacker above.

A series of those screechy snapping shots followed, as if the marksman were angry. The slugs whizzed wild, a little behind the dun. One burned hair off his rump, stinging the animal forward, which in turn saved him from a slug in the belly.

"That's some kind of gun," Fireball grunted. "Screechy like that. Scares me worse than the war ever did."

The big sorrel lunged upward, gathering himself in leaps as he plunged toward the ridge, while the dun slammed into his rear, stumbled, and kept on going.

The cover got better. Stray jack pines and junipers. Boulders. Coulees. Broken boulders. Odd strata of yellow stone.

The screechy bursts continued, but the shooter was blasting blind, catching only glimpses, hoping to score.

"I'll git down offen this sorrel now," Fireball grunted. "You git up there to the cave. You're not fit, and you need rest bad."

He slid off with surprising grace.

"To hell with that," Canada snarled, though his chest was fiery with pain.

"No. Don't be some damn dead hero," Fireball growled. "Now take this dun's lead rope and git. I'm going to circle back on foot and have a lookee at that buzzard."

They glared at each other. Canada unwilling to admit his weakness; Fireball commanding with all the force of an experienced warrior.

"Get Crowbait out of bullet range," Fireball said.

Something sagged in Canada, and his body shook with raggedy weakness.

"I'll be better off on foot than coping with that plug," Fireball said. "See you at the cave."

He ducked back up the ridge, while Canada moved heavily forward and rode clumsily over the coulees and slopes to the hideout.

Behind the sandstone slab, at twilight, Canada slid off Crowbait and landed in a heap. His weakness frightened him. He sat quietly for a few minutes and then dragged himself up. He undid Crowbait's girth and let the saddle tumble to earth. The sorrel turned around to stare.

Canada let the dun's panniers drop. He couldn't lift them. Then he dragged off the packframe and pads and collapsed against the cave wall. After he had rested a few moments, he hobbled the horses and turned them loose. There were plenty of puddles for water.

He felt sick and weak. He sprawled flat on

the rock, feeling cold but too tired to help himself. The wounds drained away his last reserves. The orphaned man — stripped of the animals he loved, the land he had settled gone, his self-esteem rubbed raw — felt blackness swarm over him. He slid into a nauseous darkness compounded as much by despair as exhaustion.

A whistle reached through the night.

A voice soft and careful. "I'm coming in Canada. Don't shoot."

Then Fireball was there, a black hulk. The foreman looked at Canada, the strewn panniers, sprawling saddle, and read the story plain.

"Find anything?" Canada mumbled.

"Some of the durndest brass cartridges you ever did see. Twict as long as any I've set eyes to. Must be a man who plumb means to kill," Fireball growled softly.

He piled a blanket over the horse trainer and began to organize their camp.

Chapter Nine

Thomas Bell stood in the window of his second-floor Billings office, watching his Northern Pacific crews work on the westbound that had just chuffed in. He pulled his pocket watch; the train was twelve minutes late.

Up ahead, men had rolled open the double doors of the green-and-gilt baggage car, and had laid a wooden ramp down to the platform. Then they led two striking horses down to the concourse — one a high black Thoroughbred stallion, sleek and powerful and in racing condition. The other, a bay mare, also Thoroughbred, with equally fine lines.

It was unusual cargo for a passenger train, Bell mused, as he watched the bustle around the coaches and Pullmans. The horses shook themselves giddily in the late sun and tested their legs on solid ground. To the rear, a switch engine, belching cinders from a firebox full of soft Montana coal, coupled itself to a private car, gilded in the grand style that bespoke opulence and power. Bell knew, in fact, that it was the car of one of the directors of the NP itself.

The engine backed the car off the train and then pushed it onto a siding that veered around the other side of Bell's office. It was time for the Montana supervisor to don his coat and greet the car's occupants.

A white-coated steward was polishing the handholds as Bell strode toward the car. Then a young lady stepped down, her sorrel hair radiant in the low sun. Her green eyes settled upon Bell and recognized him. She smiled warmly. He thought she was more stunning than ever, this thin, angular, high-breasted young widow. In spite of a lifetime of sober responsibility, Bell felt himself momentarily bedazzled. Women like Linda Reed Van Pelt never came to the rude West, nor ever crossed the path of Thomas Bell.

She held a gloved hand out to him; he took it with a slight bow. She laughed suddenly, even before she had said hello.

"I know what you're thinking. Hello again, Mr. Bell!"

Some explosion of amusement rolled out of the girl and caught Bell amidships.

"You're right; I was thinking it!" he grinned.

The man who had sired Linda Reed Van Pelt stood beside her, a full head taller, radiating steel in his strong plain face.

He's tall and thin like Linda, but there the resemblance stops, Bell thought to himself as he greeted the man and suffered his bearish handgrip. Reed had small alert blue eyes set in a rough-hewn face, with a prominent aquiline nose and a heavy jaw. He was clean shaven, but gray bristles were starting to shadow that powerful jowl.

"The mountains at last," Reed said. "I thought we'd never see them. I suppose I'll have to content myself with this distant view, because this willful daughter of mine says her ranch is in some rugged hills out on the plains." He laughed. "As long as there's some whitetails to hunt, or some elk, I'll be content all right."

"There's both, lots of them," Bell smiled as he shepherded them into his office. Reed's alert eyes seemed to absorb every scrap of data that emanated from Bell's establishment — the orderly desk, polished spittoon, clean room, and washed windows.

"Things have been going smoothly since we closed the final gap to the Pacific last year," Bell said, anticipating Reed's questions.

"I'll catch up on the NP later," Reed interrupted. "Right now, we'd like to know about Linda's ranch."

Bell sighed unhappily. He dreaded what might happen out there soon.

"You know about the rustling," he began. "And I reported that Parker almost died of a gunshot wound."

"How is he?" Linda asked urgently.

"Very gravely wounded, Mrs. Van Pelt. He's recovering at the McFarlands' — your neighbors."

"Wounded trying to help me," she said softly. "We owe him so much — we brought him these horses . . ."

"Yes you do," Bell agreed quietly. He looked at Reed, then. "No one can safely get into those mountains any more."

"My daughter is a very determined young lady," Reed replied.

"The rustling's a plague on all of central Montana. Out of control. Whole strongholds, like the Bull Mountains, beyond the law. We've got railroad detectives watching brands, and as far as I know none of the stolen beef is moving by rail. Your Herefords are probably still in there; purebloods like that are noticed," Bell sighed.

"How can they just, just *do* that?" Linda asked.

"This is still the frontier, Mrs. Van Pelt. A lone sheriff or two. Some worthless soldiers up at Fort McGinness, near Gilt Edge. And a vast, empty prairie to hide in. It's just not settled."

Reed eyed his daughter. "We're working on it. Certain people in our employ are gathering evidence and tracing the lost stock," he said.

"I'd advise you flatly not to go in there," Bell repeated.

There was a long silence.

"I respect your advice, Mr. Bell," Reed said at last.

"I'll say this," Bell argued. "Only this week a land broker approached me about buying the VP ranch and the remaining Herefords on it. He said he represented a rancher at Grass Range, name unknown. How did that broker even know to contact me? I feel in my bones the deal is connected with the Bull Mountain rustling."

"It's not for sale!" Linda shot at him. "I never knew what I wanted from life until Randy and I settled there. I want to stay, to employ Canada Parker and others, raise the best beef I can, and some good horseflesh too."

"I told Linda I don't like it," Reed grumbled. "But it's hers, her decision. I decided to join her if I couldn't lick her," he grinned. "You don't know how it is to rear a redheaded woman. She'd have her way, even if she were dealing with a Morgan or a Vanderbilt."

"Do it later, not now! Give it six months!" Bell insisted. "It can wait until it's safe."

"The man we hired isn't waiting and isn't safe," Linda retorted. "You know what he said to me? Life is never safe. It's when we think everything is safe that the roof caves in. I liked that because it's true. I don't like danger for its own sake, but I'll accept it if I must. There's not one person who comes out here to the frontier who didn't risk danger in order to reap the rewards. Well, I will too! And Dad will. We Reeds are like that."

Thomas Bell had a sinking feeling in his stomach, a vision of sudden death once again.

They left in the morning, on a buckboard driven by two smart horses, with the two Thoroughbreds tied behind.

"All I see is prairie," grumbled Reed after they had pulled out of the Yellowstone Valley.

"You'll see!" she replied. "Why don't you

count antelope?"

By midafternoon layer upon layer of wooded ridges rose before them.

"You'll be changing your mind soon," Linda said. "But before we start climbing, we'll visit with the McFarlands."

She nodded toward the comfortable white house that was coming into view. "They're our nearest neighbors and full of hospitality. And Canada will be there!"

But it was a different family they met now. "Where's Canada?" Linda asked.

"Should be at your place, far as I know," Stuart said somberly. "I sent my foreman along with him for safety, and because he's weak."

"He shouldn't be in there, but he insisted," Anne added darkly. "I don't expect ever to — I mean, don't count on anything."

James Reed stared from father to daughter. These people had none of the ebullience that Linda had described.

"Mr. McFarland. How badly have you been hurt by all this outlawry?" he asked bluntly.

Pain crossed the rancher's face, and Reed saw it. "Four men dead. My neighbor, Canada, almost killed. My foreman, Fireball Fenton in there, God knows where . . ." He ran a shaky finger through his sandy hair.

"It's no good any more. I may have to sell out."

"Dad!" Anne stared at him. It was the first time he had said it.

"Those deaths. How did they happen?" Reed persisted.

"Bushwack. That's ambush if you're not used to our western lingo. We were moving in on those missing beeves and stepped right into it." He shook his head, like a tired grizzly. "This here dimple in my arm's a souvenir."

"How are they armed?" Reed asked.

"Don't rightly know," the rancher replied. "Winchester model 73s, probably."

"No match for a high-powered rifle . . ."

McFarland stared at the financier. "If you think some added range in your huntin' rifle'll keep you safe . . ." he shook his head, not caring to belabor the obvious.

"No. I'm just weighing prospects and odds. I work with facts. Facts alone, McFarland. The more I have, the more leverage I have to bring events into my favor."

Linda was uncommonly quiet, the prospect of bloodshed having at last pierced her young optimism.

"Well, Linda?" Reed asked ironically.

They drove quietly up the wooded road and Reed at last saw the beauty of the grassy

parks, rugged slopes, and sandstone outcrops. He unpacked the rifle and shotgun,
and chose the shotgun because it was a
repeater. But the land lay peaceful before
them as the sun caught the western slopes
and shadowed the eastern ones. He began
to relax a little, yet warily studied each
hundred-yard vista ahead for its concealed
dangers.

Linda drove grimly yet stubbornly. She
had not been born redheaded to back away
from trouble.

"This is the through road to the north?"
Reed asked.

"Yes. To Roundup, Grass Range, Lewistown, and the gold camps," she replied.

"The stage goes through regularly? And
other traffic?"

"Yes, three times a week," she said.

"Then this road is fairly safe," he said.
"But once we turn off toward your
ranch . . ." The words hung in the air.

An hour later she took a right fork and
eased the buckboard down two grassy ruts
that led to the VP. The twilight gathered in
the quiet hills, and the prospect of violence
seemed remote in the lavender peace.

"We're on VP land now, Dad," she announced later. "It's home! — What there is
of it now . . ." Her elation, her love of the

West and its wilderness rose up in her, only to be tempered by the austere terror that lay upon this place.

Reed found himself admiring the rolling land and high-grass valleys. It would be a place to cut loose on one of those Thorough-breds and run down the wind. He was too used to barriers; fences both real and spiritual back East. And now this untamed land beckoned, and some homing instinct made him glad.

"You did well," he said simply, conveying some special bond between his own feelings and those of his strong-willed daughter.

They passed Hereford cows and calves grazing peacefully. They rode by a bull laz-ing on the ground. Something about it troubled Linda.

"These are your Herefords?" Reed asked.

"Yes — yes! Why, they're here! Canada must have found them!" she cried, remem-bering the days of hunting for them with the horse trainer. "I just can't believe it," she said happily.

Reed was puzzled. All his experience led him to believe that good things like this just rarely happened; there were reasons, some-times dark.

"Why are they here, Linda?" he asked soberly.

"Why, I suppose Canada found them!"

"That doesn't really make sense, does it?" he asked. "Are you sure you know which side of the fence Canada Parker's on? We're arriving unannounced, you know."

"Of course I'm sure!" Linda snapped. She plunged into a fierce silence.

Reed considered his daughter and felt her rage running toward himself. There was something in her outrage that settled his question about Canada.

"I know you're right about Parker," he said softly. "But let's think a little about why these cattle are here. You don't seem to have lost many. Who put them back? The rustlers? Are they controlling the VP?"

"We'll find out from Canada when we arrive. It's only five more minutes," she said stubbornly.

"We may meet strangers there," he said softly.

They rode up to the VP in the last light of dusk, and it was desolate. James Reed was immediately impressed with the solid comfort of the place. But there were no horses in the corrals. No lights. An uneasy silence.

They rattled into the yard and pulled up at the massive front door, shadowed in gloom.

"Canada's not here," she said. There was

a note in her voice so haunting that James P. Reed understood it at once, and understood at last his daughter's urgent need to come here.

"I didn't think he would be," he said quietly. "Ever since I saw the VP cows and calves."

"I don't follow you."

"Linda — this may be your land, but is it your *territory*?"

She stared at him.

"If it's not your territory, then Canada Parker is either hiding or . . . not alive."

"Let's get inside," she said urgently.

They moved in and bedded the horses. Linda closed the shutters. It was a soft July night and no fire was needed. She fixed a cold supper while her father wandered from room to room, enjoying the comfort of the place.

"What do we do next, boss lady?" he grinned, as he pushed back his plate. "How are you going to run this outfit?"

"I don't know," she replied. "I've never been in a spot where I was half-afraid to step out the door."

"Well, let me offer some observations and a suggestion or two," he began. "Number one, we're smack in the middle of an outlaw empire which neither law nor friends can penetrate. Two, we're in jeopardy; what they do to us depends on their whim and our skills. Three, as the rightful owner you may have something they want — a deed. There's some safety in that, and also great danger. It depends on whether someone wants to buy legitimately or just take over. Four, you are an attractive young woman and will face additional jeopardy because of it. I'm sure you understand me perfectly."

Linda colored, and clenched her hands beneath the table.

"Five, we are probably safer here than out in country neither of us knows and can't handle well. Bell, and the McFarlands, at least, know we are here. And if Parker is alive, he'll eventually find us."

"What do you suggest?" asked Linda tightly.

"Staying close. Living cautiously. Waiting to see who or what comes to our door. I'm not helpless, not with that pump shotgun full of buckshot. But more importantly, I know men, and I have a way with them. My successes have been built upon knowing men, dealing with them, plumbing their strengths and weaknesses. That, rather than the shotgun, is my real strength. The situation will clear up fast — within days. *Someone* will come here to check these cattle and the water."

"I'm sorry we came," she said raggedly.

"Don't be. I'm enjoying the challenge," he grinned. "Linda, never forget the maxim of prudent boldness. Life goes to the audacious, but not the reckless or the timid. We have great odds on our side. Not the least is the inherent weakness of all outlaws. They're failures, and they know it. Running from those disciplines and traits that build success. Industry, courage, perseverance. They're weak, despite their swagger. And as such, they can be handled — usually."

"But you're worried about the ones who can't — the mad dogs," she said.

"Mad dogs are the worst menace," he agreed. "They're unpredictable. Driven by their own demons that no one else can fathom."

He rose, stretched, and bid her good night.

Preacher sat his horse in such a way that he could peer over the western ridge and down into the VP yard. He came to this very overlook often to admire the solid buildings and his purebred stock dotting the flats southward for miles from the ranch buildings. It was an overcast day but that didn't undermine his lustful observations.

The VP was a woman he could never have

enough of. She might belong to others, but he *possessed* her, and the more he took, the more he lusted.

Now, in fact, he was absorbed by the sight of a thin redheaded woman drawing water at the pump. A surprise! She peered worriedly up at the ridges and barns and sheds, and then ducked back inside.

"Praise the Lord, I do believe my chance has come," he exclaimed. With powerful glasses he scanned the corrals. Two stunning horses caught his eye. Even at that distance he could see their sleek form and the ripply muscles that suggested blooded animals. He saw a shiny black buckboard with cushioned seats, and a pair of grays, with harness marks still upon them, as well.

It would never do to descend from the hills, so he circled around the western ridge until he hit the ranch road, and then headed straight for the log home and Mrs. Van Pelt.

He rode boldly to the door, hitched his horse, and rapped. There was a long delay, and he felt himself being studied. When at last the door opened, he confronted not a thin, angular redhead but a middle-aged man with piercing blue eyes and a massive jaw. It took him aback, if only for a moment.

"Good morning, sir," he began. "Are you the owner of this small paradise?"

Those eyes slowly scanned Preacher, settling first on his tied-down pistols and then his face.

"Not exactly," Reed said. "It is owned by another."

"I am," came a woman's voice from within. She was standing quietly in the shadow just behind.

"Well praise the Lord, I've been a-wanting a word with you for nigh on three years," Preacher said.

Reed's eyes moved to the horse beyond.

"I'm Jeremiah Jonas, though friends call me Preacher because I'm always talkin' like my daddy, who brought so many frontier folks to the Lord."

Reed smiled thinly.

"I have a small spread, nothing much, over at Grass Range, but I've always hankered to buy this one. I've seen it a time or two trailing supplies back from Billings. And this time I finally caught someone home. I guess Providence is finally easin' up on me," Preacher said.

There were no supplies on the horse.

"Oh, I've sent my men ahead, up the Roundup road. I just detoured thisaway, hankering to dicker for this nice spread, if I could just find the rightful owners home."

"It's not for sale," Linda said sharply.

"Might it be in the future?"

"No. I intend to stay and run it."

"What might be your name? Long as we're almost neighbors," Preacher asked.

"Does it matter?" Reed asked.

"Not if you feel crosswise about it. Fact is, I've a land broker in Billings trying to deliver an offer on this. Mind you, I can't pay all cash . . ."

"I believe my daughter made it clear it's not for sale."

"Well, maybe the Good Lord doesn't intend for a humble man like me to have such a nice place," Preacher sighed. "I heard tell there's some trouble up in these Bulls anyway. My woman and I, why we just steer clear o' trouble, read the Good Book by the lamp each night, and trust in the Lord. Say . . . are any of those purebloods for sale? A man might put some meat on his beeves with a bull or two."

"No," said Linda flatly.

"These bulls are already in your possession anyway, aren't they?" Reed asked suddenly.

"Possession?" Preacher was taken aback. "Now what makes you say a thing like that?"

"Nothing," Reed said calmly. "I was wondering if your spread at Grass Range is for sale? I might wish to look at it, ride up

178

there with you. A man never has enough grass to suit him."

"For sale?" Preacher's jaw worked nervously.

"How many sections is it and what are you carrying on it?" Reed persisted.

"Why, ten sections, one patented. Uh, five hundred head all told," Preacher said hastily.

"Mind if I get a description at the courthouse? I'm interested and maybe I'll just drive up there one of these days. What's your name, and brand, and how do I get there?"

"Name? Preacher Jonas, like I said. Uh, we've been slow filin'. No. I'm not sellin' neither. Lord planted me there to work and labor and build up an edifice."

"How was your calf crop this spring?"

"Fair to middlin'. The Lord provides."

"What's your brand?" Reed asked.

"Why, I do believe . . . Diamond B."

"Oh?" Reed's eyes pierced into the gray-bearded man at the door. "That's most interesting. Someone was using your brand on those bulls here. They're all Diamond B or X Ladders. Are they yours?"

"Why —" Preacher's hands grew clammy.

"What did you do with all the steers?" Reed asked.

"Steers?"

"My daughter says there's not a steer in sight."

"What did I do — Lord almighty? How an innocent wayfarer can get tangled up . . ." Preacher said.

"When did you return these mother cows and calves?"

"Return? I didn't know you had any missin'," Preacher said, recovering a little.

"Where are you from, Mr. Jonas?"

"Oh, round about everywhere. My daddy, we just kept our tent moving where the Spirit took us. Kansas railheads mostly. I don't know what yer askin' all these questions for, but you're shapin' up to accuse me of something. That's the frontier for you; a passerby gets hanged from the nearest tree before the hangmen get their facts straight."

"An interesting observation, Mr. Jonas," Reed said sardonically. "If we should change our mind about selling, how can we get in touch with you?"

"Well, that land broker in Billings —"

"No, I prefer to deal with principals. At your ranch?"

"Principals?"

"Buyers and sellers, or lessees, or whatever, not their agents. Are you representing someone with this offer?"

"No, just myself."

"Are you competent to make a down payment?"

"Oh, the Lord's been good to me, He has. As the Book says, 'Put the Kingdom first and all will be added unto you.' I do believe I've got the kingdom."

"And all has been added unto you," Linda laughed.

"Well, it's been nice to meet neighbors," Preacher said, retreating. "See you again, Mrs. Van Pelt."

"Nice horse you have," Linda said. "A Morgan I believe."

"Stout little horses. I was lucky to buy him," Preacher said.

She stared at the Bar OB Bar brand and suddenly grinned.

Preacher headed north up the slope. His stomach churned and his trigger finger itched. He'd been found out for certain. The first time anyone could finger him. That man was a menace.

Preacher rode thoughtfully, mulling his dilemma. With her back and not selling . . . the VP seemed distant. Unless — he put the thought aside.

Worse, he could hardly remove those purebloods now. It was as if he had handed the Van Pelts back their stock on a platter.

That man. No man had ever toyed with him like that. The more Preacher reviewed the sparring, the more furious he got. The man had stared right through him, sparred with him, pried him open, smiling all the while. Every question had been deadly; every comment a harpoon.

Some white rage exploded in Preacher's head. Powerful or not, that blue blood would die as easily as other men, and spill plenty of red blood and guts like common men. And with the father out of the way . . . the daughter would be easy. Easy! A little twisting. A few threats. A signed bill of sale. And maybe — an accident.

It was a task just suited for Yuma.

CHAPTER TEN

James P. Reed started to enjoy himself. This great West appealed to him, with its freedom and responsibility. He had been too long in the city, he thought. Too busy making money; not busy enough enjoying God's great world and its wild beauties.

"I'd like to buy half, if you're willing to part with it," he said to Linda. She laughed, pleased with the offer and the prospect of his company.

"It would cost you dearly," she retorted. "One dollar plus at least three months a year here every year!"

"You've sold cheap," he laughed. "I hope you won't peddle your Herefords the same way."

They saddled the horses. Linda slipped her English tack on the new bay mare; her father tried the big western saddle for the first time on one of the gray geldings that had drawn the buckboard. He liked the feel of it, except for the trot.

They rode warily, sticking to the flats within sight of the house and its safety. They examined the fat cattle, separated the better bulls from the lesser ones, and eyed the rollicking calves. Quietly, James Reed surveyed the hills every few minutes, looking for the first hint of trouble. None came. The summer sun flooded down serenely upon the greenclad hills.

"The worst may be over," he said reflectively. "When upright people assert themselves, the blackguards usually back off. Right isn't might, though. Plenty of virtuous but weak people collapse under trouble all the time. But doing the right thing does sort of armor a man; he doesn't have to answer to a guilty conscience, and if he's a believer, as I am, he knows there's some benevolent force — call it Providence if you will — helping him out in an honorable business and life. I've known some rascals on Wall Street, but what really impresses me is the number of high-minded men I've met. They're the ones who prosper in the long run. I suppose it's the same anywhere, even out here."

They dismounted at the corral.

"I'll put the horses away so you can tackle some lunch," he said.

She left him there, for the house.

The screeching shot slapped her ears just as she paused at the door. She turned to see her father, stricken, with a spreading red blotch upon his chest. She froze in terror, and another screeching shot caught him a little lower in the back, and emerged trailing a funnel of blood. He sank into the sunlit ground, upon his back. She ran. He saw her, and then didn't see any more.

"Get Fat," he whispered, choked once, and died.

She stared at him, her father, transfixed with horror as the blood widened in the dust. There was a clatter on the slope, and a rider, a banty man with a pointy black beard, rode easily downhill, grinning peculiarly as he coddled his rifle.

She fled for the house, heart hammering so fast she thought she'd faint. The shotgun was behind the door. She raised the shotgun, waiting. She heard the clopping hooves. Then silence. Then the crack of a pistol. Then silence again. Furious, she ducked into the open door, saw him staring down at her father, and squeezed the trigger. It wouldn't move. She fumbled for the safety, found it, and this time the heavy gun exploded, raising dust in front of the man's horse. He turned casually, whipped a pistol shot at her that smashed wickedly into the doorjamb. She pumped and fired again. Some of the shot hit his horse. It bucked. Her shoulder ached from recoil. He rode the wild animal until it calmed, and then spurred it northward. She pumped and fired again, and the shot sailed into the space where the man had been an instant before. Then he was out of range, climbing easily up the distant slope.

She stared wildly at her lifeless father, feeling a curtain of loneliness descending, loneliness so terrible that she knew it would never heal. All this man's genius, his love, his strength, his protectiveness, had poured out upon the clay. She kneeled beside him, paralyzed in the noonday sun, for an eternity and had no consciousness of the passage of time. And then at last she rose, weeping.

"I'm a Reed and I won't forget it, Dad," she said as some steely coldness settled into her soul. "I'm my father's daughter," she said, grasping some reality about herself that had lain dormant until then. She stared bleakly at the solid ranch that had stolen the lives of her husband and father. Yet she didn't hate it; she only resolved to keep it and to pay back its blood price.

She wasn't strong enough to lift him, so she dragged him gently away from the sun and flies, toward the barn, and left him at last upon hay, covered with a tarpaulin. She walked up the slope to Randy's grave and sat remembering him vividly, his every smile and gesture, his caresses in the night, and the timbre of his voice.

She tried to dig a grave beside Randy's, but the pick bounced off the hardpan and her shovel leaped lightly from the gumbo. She gave up.

She gathered the mare she had ridden and hayed her. She caught the gray gelding and fed him also, while she considered what to do. She had to let her mother know . . . and the Van Pelts. But that would have to wait. She was not inclined to flee East as she had done in the spring. She was here; this was her home, her dominion. She resolved to stay, using whatever weapons she could master.

The young woman who had begun this July day no longer existed. In her place, a woman of whipcord purposefulness emerged. She gathered her father's rifle and boxes of his cartridges. She paced off fifty yards and nailed a white sheet with a penciled X upon it, to a tall pine.

Then she aimed and fired. The discharge made her wince, and her shoulder hurt anew. She fired again, this time clipping a corner of the paper. Coldly she aimed until the sights were dead on the mark. There was no longer the faintest tremble in her hands. The rifle bucked and a black circle appeared just an inch from the center of the X.

Linda set down the rifle and had a closer look. It pleased her, but it wasn't good enough. She shot again. And again. The rifle bucked throughout the afternoon. Her shoulder grew numb, but she didn't notice.

After a while she decided that it was time to tackle longer distances. She shot at debris on the slopes, watching the eruptions of dust. She shot at crows, swinging her gun in an arc as she squeezed. She missed them all.

Then she strode into the big empty house and wiped the rifle clean. What next? She could get to McFarland's easily. The mare was fleet and would outrun anything, she was sure. But she didn't really want to do that; she wanted to find Canada. The trouble was, there were hundreds of square miles of wilderness, not to mention evil men who might not hesitate to harm her.

She worked through her father's effects while her mind churned the problem. There was a two-shot derringer and a box of its cartridges, plus a small telescoping brass spyglass. She put them aside. The glass, in particular, might help out here.

She yearned to be hugged. She wished Randy were there, in the big vaulting living room before a fire, hugging her until she was crushed against him. Then she wished her father could, once more, give her an amiable squeeze with that broad grin of his that he reserved for his special daughter. But he was dead. And the need persisted. Canada. She needed Canada. Once she had gratefully kissed him good-bye. Now, in a woman's way, she longed for his arms around her, safe and warm and alive.

Where might he be? Was she prepared to spend days or weeks in a wilderness, risking the elements, the outlaws, even death? Discomfort? Bad food? Poor sleep? She would. She would risk all that and more to find him. Her hope of staying here and mastering this land hinged upon Canada, and Canada alone. She knew in that instant that she loved him. Her hope of hiring him, keeping him there on the VP, had only masked love for the tall, somber man who had a little of Abe Lincoln's sadness and wisdom upon him.

"Canada Parker, here I come," she bellowed suddenly, pleased in all the curling corners of her soul that she had made her commitment. With a flip of her head that made her long sorrel hair swirl out in an electric arc, she began preparing for her leap into the unknown. She knew, in that instant, where she would look — if only she could remember how to find the place. Like some women in love, some canny intuition was guiding her, homing in across distance and time upon the spirit of her beloved. She thought she knew where he might be, though she was helpless to explain how she knew it.

She had no plan other than to ride to the niche in the cap rock where they had lunched. It never occurred to her to think it through more carefully; leave a note there or a signal that only he could interpret. It wasn't her woman's way to plot it out, nor did she know what she'd do if Canada weren't there. He would be there because she loved him.

The thought sent some elegant excitement coursing through her body, some anticipation. And for the first time that afternoon she escaped the numbing presence of death. She prepared a supper, ate heartily, finding courage within herself even as she gathered gear together.

She intended to travel light, the way a cowboy or a soldier would. She fought down the instinct to load up a second horse with everything she'd need for comfort, even luxury, in the wilderness. Her father had purchased a fine set of U. S. Cavalry bags of light pigskin, with three buckles securing each saddlebag flap. She filled them thoughtfully, with a poncho, the glass, the derringer, ammunition, matches, jackknife, and some women's things. With a burst of that genius that had blessed the Reeds, she got four ready-made horseshoes from the barn, plus some nails, a hammer, and a rasp. She wrapped jerky, salt, flour, tea, and sugar. She tied on her bedroll, and filled the canteen. She dragged it all to the corral in the gathering dusk. Then she changed into her doeskin riding culottes and the matching doeskin coat that she knew would be welcome in the cool evenings. She combed her glossy hair before the looking glass, thinking all the while of Canada. Then she lowered the wick of the kerosene lamp until it blued out, and slipped into the starry night.

The Thoroughbred mare was not accustomed to the western saddle, and side-stepped nervously in the quiet as Linda loaded on the saddlebags and extra gear. At the last minute she added a scabbard with her father's rifle and then boarded the nervous animal.

She trotted quietly out of the ranch yard, silent under the great dome of the western heavens, and was moved by this beautiful place and its fearsome cost to her.

"Oh, God," she said out loud in a clear, sweet voice, "I give you the soul of my father. Welcome him home, please, for he was upright and followed your paths. And bless this, my home, and guide me to the man I need . . . and love. Thank you . . ."

She touched her heels to the mare then, and it bounded ahead with the memories of the starting gate in its head. But it quickly settled into a steady jog over the long hills of Montana. Linda knew she had to travel east, and perhaps a little north, three miles, or perhaps four. The ridge she was looking for would be no different in the dark from any other.

She found the Dipper and the North Star, familiar friends in an alien gloom. She picked up a trail of some sort; whether made by cattle or men she didn't know, but it led east and the North Star shone firmly off her left shoulder. She followed it into the vast alive night.

She didn't know where she was going, but it mattered less to her than what was happening inside of her. The fear that at first clawed at her drained away under the friendly dome of summer stars. Some new presence emerged within her, something that harmonized with the rhythms of the night and the mare, so that she knew there was nothing to fear here and now.

She rode for an hour or so. She knew the hills were her own, yet she didn't recognize any of them. There was a ridge to the north with chimney rock on it, twin pillars of sandstone that the relentless wind had carved away from the escarpment behind them. She remembered them.

She noted the time on her father's silver watch — an hour and ten minutes of eastward walking from the house. She turned the mare upslope, through broken rock, until she rode between the pillars, ghostly sentinels in the new-moon night. She studied the country to the east and finally settled on a distant ridge, a black blur, as her goal. Then she rode onward, confident that her oneness with the night would alert her to any dangers. It was almost a mystical feeling, this sensation of being cupped under the stars by some vast benevolent spirit. She knew at last she had gone too far. She remembered it had been a two-hour ride from the cap rock to the ranch, even when checking the coulees for the missing Herefords. She backtrailed a few minutes and then cut north, sensing it was a truer line to Canada.

She didn't recognize this valley either. It gradually narrowed as it climbed toward a steep dead end that might, she realized, box her in. The last yards looked to be very difficult for a calm western horse, even more for a high-strung flatland Thoroughbred. But she drew her hand softly down the mare's neck and withers, transmitting her calm to the bay. She let the big lady pick her way over rock, leap up on shelves, jump logs and boulders, work around slabs of stratified rock with jagged edges, and finally out on the cap rock on top of the world.

Linda dismounted and walked its circumference, realizing she had climbed to this elevation at the only possible access point for a horse. At every hand, the cap rock dropped vertically away for fifty or seventy feet down to steep shoulders below.

At one point the rock bowed in sharply. She peered over the edge down upon a small flat, guarded by overhanging rock.

"Don't move or I'll shoot," said a soft voice. "You're skylined!"

"Canada!" she cried as some wild fear and joy commingled through her.

"Linda?" He was stunned. "Is that Linda?"

"Canada! I'm here. It's me!"

"Linda . . . How'd you get up there? There's no way up there."

"I'll come down and around. I knew I'd find you!"

She ran, dragging the mare behind, and leaped down the declivity with the horse stumbling behind. Far below, he ran along the shoulder toward the noise. Then he saw her, dancing down the dark, stumbling, running, leaping, until breathless, they stood before each other.

Some overwhelming shyness flooded him, and he stood speechless. But she hugged him and drew him to her fiercely, pressing him to her with all her strength. His arms closed around her then, strong and warm, and he hugged the woman who had filled his dreams for months. He was bewildered, not yet comprehending that he was loved; remembering only his forlorn yearning for this glorious sorrel girl from New York.

Linda wept freely while she caressed him and kissed him. He kissed her gently, then hungrily kissed away her tears, understanding nothing; only that this tearstained girl was clinging to him and that he felt her hammering heart pressed close to his own.

Only later, after they had led the mare into the little sanctuary and sat down against the smooth sandstone still warm from the sun, was he able to make sense of anything.

She described their return; her hopes; her father's enchantment with the ranch; the VP cows everywhere; the visit of the strange man seeking to buy; the sudden death of James Reed; the casual visit of the assassin, and the way she had chased him off. And finally her flight here.

"The mare is yours, and the stallion. My father bought them for you, for saving my life. He's sired by Audacity, out of Meadowlark. She's by Far East, out of Lady Sunset."

He was almost speechless. "You've given me running horses with that blood?" he choked. "But those horses — this mare — are worth a fortune. They've won stakes races."

"What price has my life?" she asked softly. "And yours?" She squeezed his hand.

They sat beside each other, talking sometimes, or letting the silence blanket their joy. She held his hand; her fingers tenderly explored the crease along his skull, and the scar tissue that covered it. They touched the bandaging on his chest under his shirt and traced the outline of it.

"The horses are small enough return for what you've suffered for me," she said quietly.

He said nothing, just loving the softness of her voice.

"We'll have a lot to figure out and do in the mornin'," he said at last. "I've got a partner up here, McFarland's foreman, Fireball Fenton. But he's off to Gilt Edge for a few days to talk to some people about cleanin' this up for good."

"Cleaning it up?"

"Hang 'em if we can. There's over a dozen, all told, Fireball and I figure. We've seen most riding through. But this is big country and they'd scatter easy if we did it wrong. There's usually eight or nine of 'em in the saloon at Roundup of an evening — and twenty more hardcases in there who aren't a part of this. That's where the action has to be."

"You have the evidence?" she asked.

"Yes," he said flatly. "And I'll personally deal with the one who got my horses. I know where they are — or at least were — but I can't get 'em out. Not yet."

"I think he was the one who came to the ranch door and tried to buy the VP," Linda said.

"A thin, gray-bearded fellow? Eyes that dart around? A Bible talker and all that?"

"Yes," she said quietly. "He had one of your horses. Dad sort of — well, made mincemeat of him and his lies."

"Why do you think he had my horse?"

"I recognized the brand, I think. It was a Morgan, and it had a Bar OB Bar. That could have been your CP brand, couldn't it? I mean, that's how they do it, don't they?"

"It was my horse," he said softly. "And I figure he's the ramrod for the whole bunch. He's got some brains, and just uses all those others. Now — Linda — can you talk about your father's death?"

"Yes."

"What did that one look like? A small man with a pointy black beard?"

She nodded.

He sighed heavily. "That's the one that got me, and I don't know if I'll ever get my strength back. It took something out of me that just isn't coming back with the healing."

She reached over and touched his cheek gently.

"I'm not one for falsifying things," she said somberly. "A person's always better off knowing the hard truths. Maybe you'll always be weaker now than you were, with that lung half destroyed. But you're functioning. You could still train horses with some rest breaks, couldn't you?"

"It's not the same any more," Canada said heavily. "I feel I'm at the end of the trail. I got into too many messes, had poor judgment, and now it's all come down like a heap of bricks."

"I've never heard you talk that way," she said sharply.

"You've never seen me so weak I can ride only for two or three hours before collapsing," he retorted bitterly.

She squeezed his hand, wanting to restore his spirits, knowing that the wound that ripped open his chest had also caught him in the soul and had almost shredded it.

"Have you ever thought about faith? About your destiny or what Providence has in mind for you? About God? Don't you ever feel loved?"

"No, not since I was a little boy," he said wearily.

She stared at him helplessly, powerless before forces that had drained so much vital energy from this good man.

He stood up restlessly, hobbled the mare, and checked on Crowbait.

"We've got to get in there and bury your father tomorrow," he said unhappily. "It's very risky, to say the least. I just don't know about you bein' up here getting shot at.

Don't you think you should go on down to —"

"No. I'm staying with you, my darling."

The endearment caught him in the stomach, and he turned to stare at her while she unrolled her blanket close beside his.

"Don't you think," he said tightly, "maybe I ought to sleep over yonder —"

She laughed, a melody in the night.

"Canada Parker, I'm always offending your sense of propriety!"

"Well I guess you can feel safe," he said miserably.

"Maybe I don't want to feel safe," she whispered softly. "Don't you know that I love you?"

"Linda —"

"And you love me, Canada. I know you do. Only you're afraid to say it because you think there's a barrier — class or wealth or something. There isn't. And I want to hear you say it more than anything in the world."

"Linda, I love you . . ."

She kissed him tenderly.

"I'm very tired," she whispered somberly. "So much grief in one day. And joy too. I can't stay awake another minute. . . . Good night, my darling."

She slipped into an exhausted slumber within moments, while Canada tossed and worried and troubled himself through the last of the night and didn't doze until dawn. He just couldn't get used to love.

CHAPTER ELEVEN

Canada awoke with a start. The sun was already high. He leaped out of his bedroll, fear clawing at him. He yanked on his boots and crept to the lip of their little hideout. The horses were just below, grazing peacefully. His eyes raked the woods on the other side, the rocks along the rims, the meadows.

Finally, fear still raking him, he slipped down into the meadow and led the horses into the cap-rock niche. No one had seen the hobbled animals. He was lucky, he thought.

Linda was still asleep, sleeping the sleep of exhaustion. She was a brave and resourceful woman to have weathered terror and death as well as she had yesterday, he thought. His heart tugged at him as he watched her face, with its cares washed away.

She opened an eye and stretched.

"Why did you rush out so suddenly?" she

asked sleepily.

"The horses. I always bring them in before daylight. If anyone had seen them, we'd be dead."

She was wide awake now, and threw off her blanket. The sight of her thin body, the swell of her breast beneath her shirtwaist caught and held him. She lay there warm and desirable, her hair a tawny jumble and her lips soft with sleep. He had not really seen her last night, and now the sight of her green-eyed beauty staggered him. She saw him staring, and smiled.

He became intensely aware of his stubbled face and the grime of fugitive living that covered him.

"Aren't you going to kiss me good morning?" she asked, her arms waiting for him.

He did, so gently and reverently that she laughed and pulled him down tightly.

"Canada Parker, you're afraid of me!" she whispered musically in his ear.

He didn't know what to say.

After a moment she slid out from him and combed her long hair until it crackled and sparked in the tender sun. He stared mutely, afraid of the vision, afraid that this hint of marriage, this flood of hope, this reason for living, might vanish as easily as it had come in the night. He loved her.

She cooked flapjacks over a tiny smokeless fire he built. The world and its burdens crowded in upon them as they ate; the magic of the morning faded away.

"This is the second time you'll help me bury someone I love," she said somberly. "At least the two of them can rest side by side, there on the hill."

"That may not be possible," he said. "It means being there two or three hours."

"I'd like to try. It means a great deal," she said.

They saddled quietly, aware of the dangers that shrouded the simple, necessary act of burying James Reed. Canada wished it could be avoided but knew there was no escape. The thing had to be done; it was as stern a duty as a man ever faced.

"I brought some things," Linda said. She withdrew the little brass telescope and handed it to him.

"This could save our lives," he said, excited. "You just don't know what an edge it gives us!"

She smiled and handed him the derringer.

"You keep that," he said. "That's your last resort. I'm not much a one for things like that. I'm just not that sort of man."

She nodded, loaded it, and slid it into the pocket of her doeskin riding coat.

"I brought these," she smiled, lifting out the horseshoes and tools.

"Linda! We'll be needing them for certain." He looked at her with new appreciation.

"My father taught me to plan ahead," she replied. "A little foresight will handle most emergencies."

He grinned. "How are we going to cope with the emergency at Van Pelt ranch two hours from now?" he teased, as they rode down the long slope.

"I think we'd better plan it out," she said. "Suppose we were to dig the grave first. The place on the hill — where Randy is — is not visible from the house or yard, you know. The trees . . ."

"No shovel," he said.

"I left one there, and a pick."

"What you're sayin' is that we might just do it even if some hardcases are down there."

"I think they'll be there," she said pensively. "And wondering where I am. That man — that murderer — could have killed me if he really wanted to. I wouldn't have let him capture me! I would have died first," she hissed.

"You're the only one who can sign a bill of sale or a deed," he reminded her.

"No. That's not it. That Jonas knows I'll never sell. He'd have to kill me to get the VP."

"Maybe he will," Canada said darkly. "Okay, what happens if we're spotted?"

"This mare can outrun anything here."

"On the flat," he corrected. "Crowbait doesn't have that speed, but he's got bottom and hill sense."

"I think they expected me to flee to McFarland's or Billings. And take my news with me about Dad."

"What would they gain by that?" Canada asked. "Unless maybe they just want to spread more terror around, scare people off."

"I don't know. You're giving them credit for reasoning things out in advance. Most people don't plan ahead at all. My father — often he just picked up pieces other men left behind," she said.

"You're your father's daughter," Canada smiled as he guided her along the shadowy edges of the forest, in deep shade. Fear was wound up like a clock spring in him, tightening into knots as they approached the VP.

"We'll have to go down the west slope. There's a promontory to the north where we can study it. This glass of yours may save our bacon."

He worked north until they came to the high ground, and then he eased off Crowbait and walked the last yards to the ridge until he could peer over. He felt totally drained and didn't know how he could dig the grave in his condition.

What he saw through the glass turned him cold inside.

The hardcases had simply taken over the VP. Their horses were in the corrals. The black stallion he owned but had never seen was in a separate pen. He admired it a moment through the powerful lens. There was a man at the pump. Another splitting cookstove wood. He searched further, spotted one with a ready rifle in the shade of the barn loft — a sentry.

He crabbed backward from his viewpoint and told Linda the hard news.

"Even if we dug the grave, I don't see how we'd lift your father from the barn."

"Let's dig it and try tonight," she said sadly.

He didn't want to at all, but neither did he want to protest to a woman who had just lost her father here. All it would lead to would be his own hole in the ground, he thought bitterly.

They led the horses down the long wooded slope behind the ranch buildings and onto the little glade where Randy lay. There was a fresh grave, sod heaped high, beside the other. They stared at it, slowly comprehending what had been done. Some mournful peace lay upon the place and the tall grass rustled in the midday zephyrs.

She gave her rein to him and sat down beside her father, saying her good-bye. She didn't weep this time, but only sifted the sandy soil absently through her hand while she stared out upon the blank, blue sky, and found no explanation at all that made any sense of death, or life, or hope.

He chafed at her languidness; the delay meant danger. He wanted desperately to flee. And yet, his heart went out of himself, and he experienced her own suffering and bore her burden within himself and knew that the thing called love had given him that power to share sorrow with his beloved.

It was too late.

A Morgan horse trotted into the glade, with Preacher up. Canada dug for his hog-leg.

"Horse trainer, that ain't social," Preacher said ominously. "Mrs. Van Pelt might be caught in the middle while she's payin' her respects." His hand was filled with blue steel.

Slowly Canada shoved his old navy Colt

back, while a wave of bitterness flooded through him.

"I didn't expect . . . ," Preacher began.

"You didn't expect to find me alive," Canada grunted savagely.

"Well, the Lord giveth and the Lord taketh away," Preacher intoned, his eyes feasting on Linda.

She stood and faced him coldly. "Why do you profane the sacred?" she asked. "Why do you use God's name in vain, use him for your evil?"

Preacher looked genuinely puzzled. "Why, I just came to pay my respects to Mr. Van Pelt and sort of protect your place for you. That's the golden rule, isn't it?"

"It's my father, James Reed, not Mr. Van Pelt," she said dully. "Now leave us alone."

"It's right for kin to grieve," Preacher said. "That certainly was a sad thing, a man dying sudden like that. But I imagine the chariots rolled down and gathered up his immortal soul and took him off where he's there in pure barefoot paradise."

"If you use one sacred thought or word again, I'll slap you," Linda snapped. "I'm not afraid of you."

Preacher lifted his hat and scratched his gray hair. "I guess I'll just have to turn the other cheek, then. I figgered you'd come to pay your respects proper, and that's what I'm a-doin'. Thought maybe you'd want to sell out and go back East."

It hung out in the open at last.

"It's not for sale, and I'll thank you to leave and take the others with you. All but the little one with the pointed black beard. You may take me to him at once."

Preacher chewed his beard a little. "That's Yuma. Scum no decent folks want around. The Lord sure gave up on him."

"I warned you," Linda snapped, advancing on Preacher.

Canada stood astonished by her.

"That man shot my father. Probably because you told him to."

"Mrs. Van Pelt. Your grief is makin' you not see straight. Why, I'm a sojourner here, passin' by to my own little ranch, and now you're accusin' me of all sorts of things."

"The pistol in your hand tells me otherwise," she blazed.

He put it away then, and slowly lowered his hands onto the saddle horn.

"I was just wary of that horse trainer. Now then. The Lord's my armor all right. God as my witness, I'm a-settin' here lettin' you see I'm as upright and honest as the next feller, just someone caught in the middle of your trouble."

Canada saw a flicker of uncertainty cross Linda's eyes.

"I'm no doctor of divinity, just the son of a pore old country preacher, but I know a few prayers for the dead and dyin' and I'll get off onto my knees and roll them out for the bereaved," Preacher drawled. "I myself ordered the man buried proper, when I saw the sad sight of him this mornin' when I came back to see if'n you'd considered the sale. You'd disappeared and something had to be done. I didn't know your affiliation, so I just took it upon me to read the Good Book . . ."

There was a whiteness in Linda's face, as if she had been utterly drained of her vital energies. This man now seemed to her utterly mad, or a total liar — or somehow innocent.

"Those fellers down there, now. I can't take a decent woman like you down the hill," Preacher explained. "Why, some of 'em might be rustlers or worse. I don't know who all they are; I just got mixed into bad company and I'm a-goin' to slip out from that perdition."

Linda closed her eyes in weariness. The macabre confrontation had pierced through her sorrow until she sagged.

"These Bull hills are just alive with nefarious characters, doin' evil," Preacher continued. "You'd best get out, you and the horse trainer, for your own health, or likely another innocent will soon be taken up to God almighty."

"Oh stop that!" Linda snapped.

She strode to the mare and mounted. Canada clambered over Crowbait, feeling his skin crawl, feeling Preacher's shifting gaze upon the mare, Linda's slender body, Crowbait, and himself.

They trotted urgently over the crest of the ridge and back into the clean sun and white sky, down into wheat-grass parks, running like silver streams through the darkling woods.

She reined up upon a bed of pine needles and slumped over her saddle. He leaped down and caught her as she slid off, and he held her while her body sagged into his and her legs gave out from under her. She threw her arms around his neck with her last strength and held on as if she were clinging to life itself.

"He believes himself," she said at last. "Believes himself! When I was a girl, I was taught in Sunday school that the devil is a fallen angel."

They sat down upon the soft carpet of needles. He folded her jacket into a pillow for her and drew her head down upon his shoulder as they stretched out, side by side, upon the warm ground. She lay on her side, with her face close to his, while his strong arm held her close. She slipped into something deeper than sleep.

He held her tightly beside him for hours, until the chill of evening overtook them. She awoke then, somewhat rested, and he kissed her in the twilight. She did not at first return his kiss, for her thoughts were still with her father and the terrible burial and the strange man who was the instrument of her torment.

But then she grew aware of Canada's lips, and kissed him tenderly, clinging tight.

"Yuma, the Lord abominates shoddy work. I want my hundred dollars back — in gold."

"I don't know what you're talking about," said the erect little soldier, the only person whom Preacher tolerated inside the VP ranch house.

"That horse breaker, Parker. That wasn't his ghost up there, sneakin' in with Mrs. Van Pelt. That was flesh and blood."

"The normal recourse among gentlemen, sir, is not to exact a refund, but to require that the work be completed properly," the little man smiled. "So I shall keep the double eagles."

"It's not the same. Living men tell diabolical lies about us. Heaven knows all the falsehoods and assaults upon our good names that have resulted from your carelessness. No. I want the gold, and I want you to finish the job as well."

"The task itself is not difficult," Yuma said quietly. "But your good name, sir, would remain in jeopardy."

"It's funny you mentioned it," said Preacher. "I was devining the same thing. You know, the devil is the father of all lies, and I don't wish to be lied about."

The ex-major smiled slowly. "Think of it," he said. "This whole place is yours at last; the best herd in Montana; abundance; esteem in the community of good men and pioneers. And that young woman out and around, spreading rank falsehoods about you."

"I know, I know," sighed Preacher sadly. "But it is always harder to conclude that such evil exists in the fair sex, especially in so noble an example of it."

"Two hundred dollars," Yuma said.

"Two hundred!"

"The task is new and difficult, sir. And I haven't much stomach for it, though I admit that my curiosity is aroused."

"I haven't that much gold. Sales have been rather difficult, you know. How about a draft upon my cattle."

"Ah, no, cattle are rather too portable, sir. Perhaps the half of this ranch, and an equal partnership would suffice."

"Yuma, Yuma, my friend, that is many times over a decent tithe."

"Well, I imagine, sir, that there are others who will be willing to perform this good work, but if you know of none, perhaps you will burden yourself with it . . ."

"Now don't be hasty," Preacher cautioned. "Let me meditate on this."

"I daresay you could do the job as well as I," Yuma smiled.

"No, no, not I," Preacher protested, suddenly turning pale.

"I imagine a sudden disappearance of the owner of the VP would cloud the title for at least seven years, because there would be no proof of death," Yuma said.

"Title? A title is a trifle here in the West," Preacher replied. "I'll wager ninety percent of the great ranches are held by possession alone."

"Still, it would be pleasant to know the VP won't be sold out from under you. That's where my particular skills would be at your service," Yuma said blandly. "For my price."

"Your price is too high; what upright man would pay it?"

"Ah, my friend, it is not just the existing VP we are discussing, but the one that will soon encompass the whole of the Bull Mountains, an empire of cattle, wood, land, and coal. Strike this last blow — and bear in mind that Pike and Maudie will surely succumb to a chimney fire if they aren't careful — and it shall fall to you — and us."

"It's done, then, as God is my witness," shrilled Preacher.

Yuma stroked his silken black beard. Through the kitchen window he saw the beginnings of empire. That black stallion out there, for instance. Who knows what blood it carried, and what firepower it would transmit to its progeny?

"What a lot of scum out there," Yuma sighed. "We shall shortly have to rid this establishment of the scum. There were some like that in the First Tennessee, ignoble brutes. I gave them the favor they deserved for their cowardice. A man under arms must be willing to assume any task, scale any height."

"You'd better get on with it. Time waits for no man," Preacher warned.

Yuma stood and smiled. "I shall conclude

the matter in a day or two," he said. "I daresay it will be a novelty to remember."

Preacher watched him thoughtfully as the bantam officer saddled one of the good Morgans and loaded his saddlebags and scabbarded rifle. Yuma smiled, doffed his hat, and trotted up to the little glade with its fresh grave — and the trails of two horses, only a few hours old.

"An alliance with the devil," Preacher grumbled to himself. "Now what a pity that a man is driven to such extremes. And good thing it's only temporary."

The bantam who had taken the name of Yuma to escape the families of certain Confederate soldiers where his real name was anathema, picked up the trail easily in the late afternoon.

His quarry had been walking; there were none of the marks of running horses in the trail that stretched before him. He would sight them before sundown, he supposed, as long as the trail was so clear.

So the horse breaker had survived, he thought. It didn't seem possible, but it was true that Yuma had not bothered, as he usually did, to check. On one or two occasions in times past Yuma had finished a botched job with his revolver.

He had given up any particular thought

about his victims; they were all the same to him. In the war, his rash execution en masse of his own troops tormented him for some weeks. But then it grew easier. When he was a guard at the Arizona Territorial Prison, he had thought nothing about shooting those lifers and never understood why the warden, in a rage, had threatened him with charges and had fired him. The prisoners were mere dogs, in for all their days. He had done them a favor, actually.

Yuma thought sardonically about the cowardice barely hidden behind the pieties of his new partner. The man was an odd one, deadly for sure, but with the strange quality upon him of believing his saintliness. The man seemed to be conducting a giant masquerade, more for his own benefit than anyone else's, Yuma decided.

He shrugged. It was a delusion that would come to an abrupt halt soon enough, for there was no possibility that the new partnership would last long. Yuma knew who would be the survivor; the one who didn't have a head full of illusions, or a mouthful of pieties.

Take this task now. Preacher obviously had no stomach for it but knew it had to be done. The Van Pelt woman was young and pretty, and that wouldn't make it any easier.

Yuma wondered if she'd die differently from a man. Most of those he had shot flopped and twisted unless he hit a vital area. It would be interesting to see. He would probably come up afterward to examine her. Carefully. In fact, he had to bury her some place so obscure that she'd never be found.

Yuma was faintly irritated by this job. He had never been irritated in the past, tracking men. He never considered it a serious danger: the ones he shot never met him, never saw him, never knew he was waiting to bushwack them. He never accepted a job against any man who could point a finger at him.

The tracks led northward and easterly. But the afternoon light was failing, and worse, a heavy cloud bank was imposing an early twilight. There was a danger, if he probed too deep into the darkness, not only of losing the trail but of an unintended surprise meeting that could go badly.

The trail entered a pine forest. He could see in the dimness it had been a place of rest for them. Fresh sign, still green, lay upon the needles. Yuma sensed he was close — only minutes away — but the light had by now totally failed and there appeared to be a storm brewing. He could smell it. The dampness made the sagebrush sweet in the wind.

He loved the moments before storms, when the world seemed sad and waiting for the unleashing of fury. Yuma stood in the gloom, enjoying the eddying air and rattling breezes. He wasn't a particularly happy man; in fact, he had few emotions. But there were times such as this when life pleasured him; a storm, a quarry within yards, perhaps; the pitting of his own cunning against the others. He smiled cheerfully and began to hunt a sandstone hollow or overhang into which he could duck. The Bulls were full of them. The rain would wipe out the trail, but he knew the direction and would soon pick up fresh prints in the mud of morning.

He found a good spot without difficulty and rubbed down the horse, exactly as he had done ever since officer's school. It occurred to him that the tracks were heading toward Pike and Maudie's. He couldn't fathom why Parker was going that way, but it made no difference. In fact, it would be rather a stroke of luck. That chimney fire that he and Preacher knew would burn out Pike some day might just destroy all evidence of everything, including Pike's guests. Delightful! He would follow them there and cremate them all, along with that filthy building and the whole vile place.

It would be doing Pike and Maudie a favor. They lived such miserable, filthy lives that they would be happier six feet under, Yuma concluded. That was the way it had always been; he really did people favors. Those soldiers, for instance. They would have been branded cowards and lived out their lives in shame. Those lifers. Those others. He wondered if the world would see it his way. Their suffering had stopped; he had delivered them from pain and hopelessness.

The rain came in gusts, sometimes whipping spray back upon him in his hollow. But he enjoyed it. The lightning followed and smacked down with a screeching roll of thunder. The noise pleasured him, though it upset the Morgan. Yuma sat contentedly, puffing on his pipe while the screeching lightning exploded around, sending little thrills up his spine. Tomorrow would be an excellent day.

CHAPTER TWELVE

They were miles from the cap-rock niche and miles from Canada's hideout cave when the rain rolled down on them. There was abundant shelter in the Bulls, but finding it on a jet-black night would not be easy.

He shrugged into his slicker and she pulled her poncho over her head. But their bedrolls were getting soaked and it was not going to be a pleasant night, even though it was July and warm.

They pushed on, completely lost, with only sporadic sheets of lightning to guide them. They stayed low; the ridges seemed to catch the forked bolts that crashed through the night.

The earliest settlers in that country had taken advantage of the pocked and hollowed sandstone cliffs to build dugouts and shelters, useful as line camps for cowboys. One such structure of logs, set hard against an overhanging cliff, caught Linda's eye. She yelled at Canada over the howling spatter, and they trotted toward it, or where she thought it was. There was a lapse in the lightning and they groped in blackness until finally the next sheet of white illumined the place fifty yards to the right.

It was more than they had hoped for. Beside the building was a pen where the horses could shelter beneath a deep rock overhang. The building itself used the same overhang, with a rock wall dividing off the corral.

They unsaddled gratefully in the lee of the overhang and found a rear door into the building itself. The black was dense until Canada struck a big lucifer, and they glimpsed a clean but dusty interior, a crude but effective fireplace built into the over-hang, and some dry wood. These places were used mostly during the terrible Montana blizzards, and no one ever used them without immediately replacing the dead-wood for the next emergency.

"I think this is yours. We're still on VP land and I think it was a line camp of the previous people — the Buzhardts?"

"It looks like their solid work, doesn't it?" she said gratefully.

Canada soon had a fire blazing. On a night like this he wasn't concerned about being seen. Linda pulled off her poncho and squeezed water from her sopping strings of hair. They opened the bedrolls where the niggardly heat of the fire would dry them.

The shingled part of the dugout leaked, but back under the overhang it was dry and pleasant. There was a rude bed there of wood and canvas, with a straw tick.

Linda saw Canada staring furtively at it, and laughed huskily. "Canada Parker, I'm still offending your sense of propriety!"

But this time he surprised her.

"I love and want you," he said simply. "There's a lot of marriages on the frontier that don't get formalized until some preacher comes along. What counts is whether the promises given and received are real, are sacred," he said softly.

She came up to him, her eyes sparkling, and took his hand.

"Are you proposing?" she asked softly.

Canada swallowed, as if fighting back something.

"I'm just a horse trainer with no horses," he said harshly. "Shot up, weak as a pup, and out of a different universe from you. I don't rightly want to take advantage of this here situation or your notions."

The words hung in the air and there was only the crackle of wood and the dancing shadows to animate the room.

She said nothing for a long time. In fact her mind drifted from this rainy night and she was remembering joyous nights with Randy, voyages of discovery, feelings she missed now and was tempted to seek here. Then her thoughts focused again on the rain and the man before her and she felt a fitness, some rightness in his decision, though not in the reason he gave.

She smiled and looked up into his troubled gray eyes. "I love you, Canada," she whispered. "And I want to be worthy of your love. There's a proper season for all things, a time to sow and a time to reap, and a time to mourn. A time to grieve for the ones I loved."

Her quiet dignity reached out to him with its promises for the future, and he secretly was sorry he had belittled himself. He knew, somehow, that whatever his poverty and misfortunes may have been, he had his own riches — a deep integrity to give to her, a transcendent love for her, and skills that could earn him a living for her. There would be a right time if he kept faith with himself — and they got out of this murderous mess.

She broke the spell suddenly, digging into their spare supplies for food. There wasn't much. Jerky, flour, sugar, salt. She began some crude biscuits, which they could wash down with tea.

"Tomorrow," Canada said pensively, "we'll check the cave for Fireball. We left it two ways. He'd either be back soon — by now — or he'd come after he got the Cattlemen's Protective Association into an armed group capable of cleaning up these hills. Frankly, Linda, it's a vigilante force."

"Whatever it is, I hope it succeeds."

"It's the only law we've got. Each freeholder protectin' what he's got with the best weapons he can muster. There's something right about it, especially when the lawmen or courts aren't worth a can o' beans."

"We could wait here," she said. "I like this place," she grinned at him.

"No. All these old places are dangerous for us. We've either got to keep travelin' or hiding in a spot so wild and woolly that we're plumb out of sight."

"Let's travel, then."

"That's what I'm thinking. I've a mind to go up to that Sanders outfit and talk to those two. They're a sight — I should say a fright. But now that the hardcases are down at the VP, maybe we can dig out some more facts — where all those cows are stashed. Where my horses are now. Who's in it. Those two Sanders — Pike and Maudie —

they're just being used, is all."

"Canada — when this is over, what do you want? To go back to your own ranch?"

He thought hard, or pretended to.

"I don't rightly know," he said slyly. "It sort of depends on whether I get me a filly to break."

"I thought you never broke horses; only trained them."

"Well, it depends on the horse. Some just need breakin'. If they sass you, you've got to be stern for their own sake. Who'd want a filly with notions of her own? Why, it'd be downright unsafe!"

She started to say something, but bit her tongue.

"If the rider is kind, the horse is usually good-mannered," she laughed, breaking into her melody of chuckles.

They ate, talked, and joked. He insisted she take the bed, so she rolled up in it while he stretched out on the clay floor and listened to the gusting rain. But then, in the dark, she pulled the tick and bedroll down beside him and fell asleep with her hand on his chest and her fingers languidly upon his wound, somehow transferring a healing strength into his shattered body.

The next morning they rode north toward Pike and Maudie's, with the smell of sagebrush pungent after the rain. Canada was uneasy; they rode cautiously along the edges of forests, never skylining themselves, never in the open for more than seconds. The warm earth was soft with water, leaving an unwinding trail of hoofprints behind them.

In the late afternoon they reached the foot of the palisaded mesa that hid Canada's horses. They paused at an overlook amid jumbled stone, and Canada crawled up to the cap rock where he could study the whole sorry Sanders place with his glass. There was nothing. No signs of life. The door of the house banged in the breeze. No horses. The bunkhouse door was open, flapping in gusts. A good sign, Canada thought. Yet he was unhappy, and turned often to study his backtrail with its deep prints. Nothing.

He backed away and returned to Linda and the horses.

"We'll go on in," he said. "I don't imagine the hardcases liked hanging around this pigsty any more than anyone else would."

"Is it really that bad?"

"It is, from what I've heard tell. I imagine we'll get a lesson in the ways people lie to themselves and excuse themselves."

She shuddered suddenly, aware of the narrowness of her past life. Clean young people her age, polite and ambitious and worldly.

She was about to meet some who would be entirely new in her experience.

He ground-tied Crowbait, but the mare had to be tied to the hitch rail. A middle-sized man answered his banging, a man in stocking feet, gummy dungarees, and week-old beard.

"If yer lookin' to sell something, I ain't buying," he muttered, staring suspiciously at Canada and Linda.

"We're your neighbors, Mr. Sanders. We'd like to light and set a spell," Canada replied, using the old western hospitality formula.

"The kitchen ain't what it should be. Maude never does anything," he grumbled. "What's yer business? I'm so busy I ain't got time just for palavering."

"May we come in?" Linda asked.

"Oh, might as well," grumped Pike.

She shuddered at the stink of the place.

"County taxes are so high it just don't pay to keep the place up the way I should," Pike explained. "They just haul away all a man can earn."

He offered them nothing and they were grateful not to have to refuse.

"I hear tell you have your outfit rented," Canada began.

"I did have, but that Grass Range outfit just skipped out without a howdeedoo, and owin' me over a hundred dollars, too," Pike whined. The shadows of evening deepened the fatty ridges of his jaws and neck.

"Running any stock?" Canada asked.

"What business is it of yers?" Pike asked belligerently. "I've had so many head in my day I couldn't even count 'em. Spread's too much for one man and half-a-woman."

"We're looking for stray VP cows, and I'm looking for some CP horses," Canada said. "This is Mrs. Van Pelt. I'm Parker. She runs purebloods, Herefords. I'm looking for a mess of horses."

"Horses come and go. They drove a bunch through here t'other day."

"Range horses? Mustangs?"

"I don't rightly know. I was at my desk doing my accounting — takes me hours, you know. Never did set an eye to 'em."

"Where's Mrs. Sanders? I'd enjoy meeting her," Linda said.

"Sleepin' it off, the way she does ever afternoon," Pike explained. "She's about ninety percent of my problem here. I hafta do her work and my own."

"I'd like to know a bit about this Grass Range outfit," Canada said. "Now whose might that be?"

"Jonas. Thin, gray-bearded fellow. Very respectable man, I reckon, only he ain't paid me proper yet, and that's sure slowed up my plannin'. But he'll do it. That man knows the Bible like a saint, almost."

"He had a pretty big crew, I imagine."

"He shore did. Tough fellows, too. Maybe a dozen or fifteen. I never did keep tabs. They was always complaining about my outfit but never lifted a finger to fix 'er up."

"Pike, how many head were they running?"

"Well, I don't rightly know. Lots. This place — well, you know. I haven't had time to patent any or prove it up, so I just run the northern half of the Bulls. She's one of the biggest outfits in Montana, I'd rightly say."

The last light faded, and Canada felt anxious to break away into the clean and safe dark.

"Well, that's something to go on," he said. "I suppose that bunch is up at Roundup a lot."

"You bet. They pretty near live at Grizzly Bear's saloon. I never cottoned much to it myself, but they beat a regular highway from here to there."

Canada stood and Linda rose as well.

"Don't go. I hardly never get to talk to anyone. That Grass Range outfit, they was hardly civil."

He scratched a big phosphor and lit the kerosene lamp on the table.

"Don't go. Maybe we can rustle up some grub, and maybe that woman here can do some cooking. A man could shore use a square feed now and then."

He grinned glassily at Linda. The orange light sank into the filthy kitchen and disappeared. Linda stared at the greasy dishes piled high in the drainboard, the clutter of gum and crumbs on the table before her, and the rubbish stamped into the floor.

"I'm sorry Mr. Sanders. This is not a kitchen I wish to cook in."

Pike's eyes fell. "Well, you're usin' up my kerosene," he retorted. "I thought maybe you'd like to repay."

She threw back her head and laughed. A melody of laughter rose up out of her, cascading through the old house.

The screeching snap of a rifle shot, the shattering of glass, and the whip of lead into the very space Linda's head had occupied a split second earlier, before she was overwhelmed by Pike's grumbling, exploded upon them.

Canada heaved himself toward her. They fell on the stinking floor as the next screeching bullet shattered glass and pierced straight through Pike's skull. The grubby rancher died wordlessly, slumping across the table, smashing the kerosene lamp to the floor where flames licked out in an arc upon the filth there. A third shot, fired blind into the shadows of the kitchen, splintered wood inches from Linda.

"We've gotta get out," Canada grunted. "It's burning. Those shots. I'd know them anywhere."

Linda stared in terror at him, at the flames, at the weaving shadows, at Pike Sanders with a hole in his head. She screamed.

"That first one was meant for *you*," Canada rasped. "For *you*!" He couldn't believe the truth of it.

They crawled toward the living room. A shot — from a higher angle — raked the floor where they had just been. More peppered the kitchen, whining through windows, careening into stovepipe, rattling through dishes. The fire curled up the walls and into the porch area. A window burst in the darkened living room.

"Pike?" a woman called. "Pike? Is that you? What in tarnation?" A slug exploded in the dark of her room, and she screamed. It was an eerie sound that sent chills through Linda.

The horses were on the wrong side! the

side where the bushwacker was hunkered down, spraying lead at will into the flaming building. The side with the door. Flames broke through the roof, turning the log building into a beacon that illuminated all the ground for a hundred yards around.

The horses, terrified, jerked free, plunging into the darkness. Too late, Yuma saw them race off, turn to stare, and edge out upon the night. He shrugged. No one could reach them now, providing anyone had survived the holocaust of fire and lead. He shot contentedly through windows. All the rooms were day-bright inside. No one could move without his knowledge. Too bad he wouldn't get to see how the woman died. It had interested him. He'd caught her, for sure. He saw her head fly back as he fired. Right between her pretty eyes.

"We can't get out," Linda cried as smoke choked them where they lay. Ash, live embers fell on them and they slapped the coals off. Canada was dizzy with heat and the terrible air they were breathing, sulphurous and thick.

"Air's best at the floor," Canada gasped. He began to sweat. He crawled a few feet and found a stream of cooler air being sucked toward the kitchen. He dragged Linda to it.

"Linda, can you hear me?" he barked.

"Yes," she said weakly.

"If we stay here we'll die for certain. If we get up and run, we'll probably be shot. But we've a better chance running. The only chance. And those weaving shadows might give us a chance."

She nodded. A beam collapsed, sending up a shower of light.

"When the next collapse like that comes, run," he barked. "Those sparks — it'll blind him a moment. Run for the back door and away from him."

She nodded, coughing terribly.

"Hold on!" he cried. "Don't let go. Don't go to sleep!"

She shuddered. Felt an ember smolder her hair. The bedroom roof caved in, sending up a pillar of sparks like an Independence Day celebration.

"Now!"

They scrambled, burning, smoking, back through the main room and toward the door at the rear. It was wedged. Canada shouldered it and they fell through into the night, gasping for clean air.

"Roll!" he rasped, and they rolled away from the inferno still shielding them from the bushwacker.

"Get your breath a moment," he gasped.

"Then we run. Zig and zag like rabbits. Hear?"

She did, sucking in air, gulping it down.

The flare had died down and they would momentarily be visible again.

The shot screeched in sooner than Canada expected, while they were still kneeling. It raised mud just between them.

"Run!" he cried. They did. The girl flew. He zigged, she zagged. A shot snapped by. She leaped sideways. Another shot caught her calf. She screamed and fell, clawing ahead. He grabbed an arm and dragged her, dipping sideways as another shot screamed into her culottes, just off her hip. He fell into something; a hollow full of blessed night, and pulled her in. A screeching bullet whipped just above.

She lay shaking in the momentary safety. He studied the situation — they could crawl along this dip just below firelight. Some commanding calm reached into him. They were alive. They had a minute or two before the killer moved in.

"Crawl, Linda. Come on."

She followed him, crying. "I'm a Reed," she gritted, and he didn't understand her at all. There were no more bullets. That meant the man was moving in.

"Hurry!" Canada begged.

The dip emptied into a shallow coulee, low enough to move at a crouch.

"We're going to make it, Linda."

"My leg isn't working," she wept.

He saw dark shapes moving ahead.

"Crowbait!" he hissed.

The horse paused.

"Come!"

It came warily, dragging its reins. The dim bulk of the mare drifted behind, reins broken.

"Can you make it?"

"No," Linda wept. Waves of undulating pain rolled up her leg. Her boot was full of blood and she was growing fainter by the second from the loss of it. She was almost paralyzed.

"I'll carry you," Canada growled, uncertain whether he could. He was far beyond the end of his own rope. His chest ached frightfully.

A burst of sparks exploded upward as the roof caved in upon the Sanders house. The horses backed off nervously.

He dragged Linda, stumbling, to the mare and lifted her over the saddle. The nervous animal skittered sideways. The fire, smell of blood, clumsy mounting all terrified her.

Linda hung to the saddle horn, lying sideways over the saddle. "I can't," she wept.

"Go! Get into the dark!" Canada rasped, slapping the mare across the rump. The horse lunged ahead, mercilessly bouncing the girl lying across the saddle.

A man appeared around the house, peering into the dark. The roar of the blaze and bouncing shadows kept him from seeing Canada or Crowbait for a moment.

Canada, using his last strength, heaved himself onto his gelding and gathered up the trailing reins even as another screeching shot pierced the night.

He caught the mare's broken rein as he trotted past. Linda hung on somehow, barely conscious. A shot racketed the night, but the little man, silhouetted by fire, was shooting blind.

Canada walked the gelding. If Linda fell, neither of them had the strength to get her back up again. He picked up a trail leading toward the palisaded mesa, climbing steadily until he could look down upon the inferno below. There was a three-quarter moon. The tracks of the two horses, deep in the wet earth, a highway for trackers, strung out behind them in the white light.

Linda was silent behind him, and he wondered if she were even conscious, hanging on through some primitive force of will. He sagged dizzily into the saddle, still gasping for breath, and with every gasp his injured lung howled.

They climbed a narrow defile through the palisade itself, boulder-strewn, and then descended the cleft and into the peaceful park. He saw at once that some of his own horses were still there — the young stuff, foals and mares and yearlings. The saddle horses were gone. He called out. Some of the mares knew him and stopped their uneasy retreat. He led Linda into the middle of the band and stopped.

He dropped off Crowbait and eased Linda to the grassy ground, cool and silent. He had to pry her hand loose from the saddle horn, so tightly had she clung to it. She watched him through tearstained eyes, too exhausted to talk.

He untied her boot and found the calf terribly swollen, with a large wound that barely missed the bone as far as he could judge in the pale light. Both entrance and exit holes were caked but still bled slowly.

He bound the wound carefully, using strips from a clean flannel shirt in his pack. Then he eased her boot on again, unlaced, until it formed a further shield against more injury.

He lifted her head until the tangle of sorrel was in his lap, and urged her to empty the canteen, to replace as much of the lost body fluids as possible. He drained his own, remembering how the heat of the inferno had sucked the liquids right out of his body. The horses watched curiously.

He wiped her face with a moist rag, and she smiled up upon him, still too stricken with shock to speak. The night breezes whispered and some of the mares began cropping grass. He could see the shod tracks of Crowbait and the mare leading across the moist meadow and mixing with the milling, unshod tracks of these twenty or twenty-five animals. He glanced uneasily at the defile where he felt certain the killer soon would come.

He found some thong among his gear and cut off a piece, tying each end to the mare's broken reins to make a continuous loop that Linda could hang on to. Involuntarily, his eyes jerked toward the defile, fearful of what might soon enter this peaceful park.

He could shoot — empty his old Colt at the man. But it would be futile. Better to flee, hide, avoid confrontation with a skilled hardcase. Linda had a rifle and he'd use it if necessary. But he knew the odds.

Every minute counted. Every second of rest helped them both but put them into increasing jeopardy. They rested as long as they dared, and then he decided to hunt for the other exit, the one he discovered the time he was shot at, off to the south.

"Linda, we've got to move," he said urgently.

She understood.

He lifted her up, and this time she made it over the saddle. She groaned when new waves of pain rolled up her leg, but said nothing. Canada stood admiring her a moment, this strong, uncomplaining, courageous and loving young widow.

He led Crowbait on foot. Things looked different in the dark, but he worked his way along the inner palisade, confident he could find the place. He remembered then, with dread, that the defile had dropped several feet into the grass. Crowbait had taken it in stride, one gathered leap upward. But the mare? And Linda half-conscious upon her?

He found the spot. Some of the broodmares stared at him, but others stared the other way, their ears cocked toward the north entrance. Urgently, Canada spurred Crowbait upward into a graceful leap, hoping the mare would follow. She didn't.

"Spur her, hit her on the rump," Canada hissed. "You've got to; he's coming."

"Canada," she cried, trying with all her strength.

But the mare balked.

"Hang on, then," he gritted, uncoiling his braided reata. He dropped the loop over the mare unceremoniously, dallied around his horn, and spurred Crowbait. The mare dug in until the rawhide rope threatened to snap, then in a bounding leap that almost unseated Linda she jumped gracefully onto the ledge and into the secrecy of the defile.

At that same moment, the man called Yuma rode into the high park from the north.

CHAPTER THIRTEEN

The man who called himself Yuma cursed himself for not shooting the horses when they stood at the hitch rail beside Pike's kitchen.

That was always the first consideration: cut off all avenues of escape. But some southern instinct for good horseflesh had stopped him. In fact, he coveted the mare the girl rode. Even from his vantage point he had seen the horse was a sleek, blooded, costly one with speed written on her.

He had selected a good bushwack point behind some stones partially upslope from the house. He had a clear view into nearly the whole kitchen. He was high enough to cover all the ground beyond; there was no escape. Resting the barrel of his finely wrought rifle on the rock, he could scarcely miss.

All had gone well at first. He had intended to do them the favor first, and then burn the place down. But old Pike, sitting in the kitchen, had fallen into the lamp and the fire had started that way.

He had been puzzled at first when he glimpsed two people escaping. Pike was dead; he had seen him slump over the table and knock the lamp over. The girl, too. Her head had flown back as he shot. He had seen it clearly through the window. He thought it was Parker and Maudie. But Maudie? She hadn't the strength to go fifty feet. It was infuriating.

Yuma rode quietly into the high park of the mesa. The tracks in the soft ground were clear enough in the moonlight. He had picked them up at once after circling the blazing building.

He remembered the military textbooks he had studied so diligently at the Citadel. Strike when your enemy is retreating; don't let him regroup. Make his weakness work against him by keeping pressure on him. Make the final effort, the last push, and triumph over him.

Yuma coolly cataloged what he knew. Parker was obviously still weak from his near-fatal wound. The girl — if that is who it was — had been hit in the leg, probably. He had seen her crab along on the ground with a useless limb. She would be weak and in shock. Both would have been further weakened by smoke and burns and heat. Their escape route was bared by the soft earth, so that even moonlight trailing was easy. It certainly wasn't the time to let up and sleep.

He wasn't concerned about being shot at; Parker had only the old pistol that he could scarcely use. And the girl . . . a cipher as far as danger went. Yuma decided he would be a bit cautious nonetheless. Some military instinct, inculcated so thoroughly long ago, ensured that he would never be truly off guard. Well, he thought, he'd get to see how a woman died after all.

He reined up for a moment in the high park, studying the grassy flat and the shadowy palisades. The mares and foals were still here, some of them staring at him. Some nervous yearlings trotted restlessly away. The shod trails led directly to the center of the park, but he didn't like that. He would be an easy mark from the shadowed cliffs. Even a pistol, resting on something solid, could do damage at any range inside this place.

Yuma was certain they were here. Where could they go in this cul-de-sac? They could perhaps abandon their horses and crawl up the palisades to safety, but they would be fools to abandon their mounts with her unable to walk. Surely, then, they were here.

He tied his gelding to a juniper, withdrew his rifle, and walked quietly into the field, ready to dive to earth. The tracks soon mixed hopelessly with the others, and not even the moonlight could help him separate them all. He eased back to the sheer palisades, then, and decided to circle the perimeter of the park. They would be somewhere in the shadows, nursing their wounds.

Yuma moved like a wraith, cleaving to shadow, silent as a hiss in the night. An hour passed. He studied each cleft, slid along the facades in shadow. He reached the end of the shadowed walls and crept cautiously along the ones on the far side, white in the light. There was nothing. He stirred a rabbit once, and whirled to shoot.

Irritably, it occurred to him that they had slipped out the way they came in; he had left the trail back to Sanders unguarded. He ran, then, for several hundred yards until he reached the exit. His horse was there, quiet, with a leg cocked up. There were no prints going back. So they were in here, somewhere, perhaps in some wallow out in the middle, well fortified.

He would have to wait for day, as much as it galled him to do it. Still, he was a soldier and an officer. Even while he made a dark camp in a hollow where he could command the exit defile, his mind was at work. Somewhere in the sun he would pick up clear prints in the muddy earth. And then he would move swiftly upon his quarry. They needed rest and couldn't possibly go far. The bantam wasn't much for bivouacking. In fact, he didn't really know how luxury loving he had become, or how soft. All he understood was that the chill night air was uncomfortable, that he lacked a soft bed, that he felt unwashed and greasy. Damned if he wouldn't revenge himself for all this tomorrow.

Canada paused after a few minutes, so tired he could barely sit his saddle. Linda weaved silently behind him, clinging with both hands to the horn. She was about at her limit. He was on the last of his reserves. The tracks rolled out behind, fresh in the wet earth, relentless flags of passage. It irked him. They were there, pointing the way, no matter what he did. He was in trouble if he stopped; in trouble if he continued. There was a point, not far ahead, where Linda would fall off, a dead weight he could no longer lift.

He searched for rocky ground, or slopes covered with brown needles, and sometimes he managed fifty or sixty yards without leaving a visible track. But it was no good. He was always forced back upon the moist earth. His efforts would delay the killer for only a few moments.

Canada racked his head for an answer, but there was none. If that was true, he decided, then the best hope was to fort up and rest. They had Linda's high-powered rifle, a little food, and empty canteens. The water was easy. He had passed pools of clear water in sandstone hollows all night. To his right was a box canyon, hemmed in by high cliffs of wind-carved sandstone. He rode into it, seeing numerous ledges, overhangs, and caves that might be defensible. They rode upslope toward the canyon's end. He selected a hollow midway up that commanded the whole canyon below, high amid boulders, shelf rock, and juniper.

He studied it after they had reached the place. There was grass for the horses, the safety of ledges and overhangs, and comfort.

"We're home, Linda," he said softly, lifting her down. She hung on to him half-consciously, and he stumbled to a place beneath an overhang and rolled her into her blankets. He was desperately tired, but his nerves were raw with the potential danger. He forced himself to prepare. He drew the rifle from the scabbard, and cartridges. He stumbled downslope with the canteens and filled them in a shining pot of water in the stone. He led the horses there and let them drink. He undid his lariat and rigged a picket line that would allow them to graze safely behind cover. He fought off sleep a few minutes more, deliberately studying the approaches, the cover, the dangers. He was no soldier, but he would use what intelligence he had.

Satisfied at last, he dropped beside the woman he loved and was asleep in moments. It was beyond him to keep watch. He only wished he could trust God the way Linda did, but his orphaned heart just wouldn't let him.

He awoke to a feeling of danger. The sun was high — too high. He had meant to start his guard at the gray of dawn, and instead it was midmorning. He lay still, but alert. The horses were both staring down the valley, ears cocked. He turned to look at Linda, still asleep, her face gaunt and shadowed with gray. A part of her leg was visible, and it was black and lavender clear to her knee, so great had the concussion been.

"Linda," he said in a low voice. "Trouble's comin' again."

She looked up at him with green eyes full of pain.

"Linda. I'm going to use your father's rifle. I've got to do it or we'll not make it. I've never shot a man before, but it's him or us."

She nodded slowly. The pain she had escaped in sleep now ravaged her until she clamped her jaw against her teeth.

"I can't make the pain go away," she gritted. "But I can accept it. Make myself live with it."

He turned to her, amazed. It was something he had done once or twice. Once when he had bellyache so bad that he thought he was dying, and he couldn't take it any more, he had told himself firmly that he wasn't getting any deader from it, so maybe he could just accept it, quit fighting it. He did, and the pain subsided. And now he saw her doing it, mastering it with an iron will.

"Give me the pistol," she said. "There's a little hole between the rocks that I can shoot through without being seen."

She dragged herself over to it.

"Pistols are for close work," Canada cautioned. "Can't waste it on long shots. You'll only give yourself away."

He wished he could get to the horses and

tie them behind rock, saddled and ready. He was considering it when he saw movement below, along the east wall of the box canyon, deep in shadow. At first he thought it was his imagination. He strained to see — it was nothing. A bird popped up down there. . . . A dart of movement again, cutting behind junipers. All in an instant.

"He's there," Canada growled.

"I'll know him," Linda said wearily. "It's the same one."

"Have some jerky. Food will help you," he counseled.

"Not hungry. I've got a fever."

Canada saw movement again but not at the juniper copse he was watching. This time it was among boulders thirty yards closer.

"My God," he whispered. "He's close enough to rush us."

"I'm ready," Linda said, feeling the derringer in her pocket.

The hunting rifle was a single-shot bolt action. Canada knew he'd have to make each shot count. He could have no more than three — probably two — in a rush. He trained it upon the next obvious cover, ten yards closer. The man snaked forward and Canada squeezed his shot. The man's hat flew back as the blast racketed down the box canyon. Canada loaded and aimed for a bit of exposed blue fabric at the base of a rock. He fired and the slug screamed off, furrowing the sandstone just above the blue, which disappeared instantly. Canada jammed another cartridge home shakily. Hands sweaty. He hated it.

A screeching shot barked from below, but seemed to go nowhere near. Then the horses pivoted sharply into the shade of a boulder, and Canada saw that the mare had an angry red streak across her stifle. She bucked; the picket line snapped, and the horses bolted uphill, through juniper and a tangle of stumps and boulders. They were almost impossible targets, and Canada was grateful. One more screeching blast racketed uphill, missing the phantom animals.

Then there was silence. It grated on for seconds, then minutes, then into jagged eternities, each a bundle of tension. Nothing. The sun reached zenith and baked the box canyon. Canada eased back into shadow beneath the overhang. Linda drew back to shade.

"I don't think he's gone," Canada said. "This waiting's worse than running, though."

"I couldn't move much anyway," she said somberly.

"I figure it thisaway. He's had a taste of lead. He knows we'll shoot now, not just run. He thinks he's got us boxed in now and he'll wait us out."

"Well he does, doesn't he?"

Canada looked closely at the bluffs that formed the head of the canyon. They rose vertically but were deeply fissured. From the steeply sloping shoulders to the rimrock was never less than fifty feet.

"He might at that," Canada agreed, "unless there's an exit behind the overhang here we can't see."

He studied the cap rock carefully, forcing his eyes to examine the line where rock met sky, segment by segment.

"He might just try some high shots, or try to ricochet some lead under here."

"I haven't seen anything move," Linda said. "He has to be there; he can't just fly up to the rims."

The tense watching extended into the silence of the afternoon. Nothing. They ate jerky and sucked on their canteens.

"At least you're resting," Canada said. "But I don't know how we'll get out . . . Linda . . . if we don't make it —"

He sighed, and she looked up at him somberly.

"I just — I want to ask you. You see, I love

you and I'd like —"

The screeching shot rattled down, not from the ridge across, but from a promontory to their extreme right, jutting from their own canyon wall, a point that left them utterly exposed. It smashed into sandstone inches from Linda's eye, spraying her with shards of rock. She cried out, even as a second screeching shot slammed into Canada's holster, exploding fragments of lead into his thigh. He grabbed Linda by the shoulders and dragged her back, uphill and around a soft bend, while yet another vicious slug mashed into the shaded stone where they had been, spraying chips at them.

They were safe for a moment. She stood up flat against the cliff and saw his dungarees turning red around the mangled holster.

"Canada," she wept, "you've been hit."

He saw the blood, but knew he was moving without trouble.

"Scratched is all. Hang on to that pistol!" he barked. There was a crack in the rock forming the soft bend that protected them. He eased up and peered through it, and found himself staring up toward the promontory and what might be the side of a man's head there. He slipped the hunting rifle into the crack in deep shadow, rested it solidly on rock, and fired. There was a tiny flick of movement up there. He fired again, this time at the base of a gnarled pine.

"That'll hold him for a bit," he growled bitterly. "Linda — we're going to get out of here over the top — somehow."

She stared upward in dismay.

"I'm going to look. Stay in the shadows, honey. Right here you're safe from above and both sides, and you've got the pistol for anything in front. And don't shoot me when I get back. Take aim deliberately and you'll do best."

She smiled suddenly. How she managed it, he'd never know, but she did, and for a moment she was her old self, green eyes sparkling.

"The answer is yes," she laughed.

He gulped. The question so rudely interrupted returned to mind. He grinned and doffed his hat.

With a lighter heart he crawled uphill from their porous fortress, squirming low behind boulders, skidding around heavy clumps of sage. He wanted a look back above their lair. What he saw disheartened him. More vertical cliffs. But there did seem to be a deep vee near the promontory that would prevent the man from circling down on top of them somehow.

There was one other cleft, the other direction, toward the head of the box canyon, that caught his eye. There was no knowing where it went or what would be in there. He could see the first fifty feet or so up it. It ascended sharply, a staircase of sorts, with shelves of native rock. It was a chance.

He could see the horses high on the shoulders, just below the rock that boxed the canyon. He would have to get them somehow. Linda had to have one. There were at least a hundred exposed yards from their protected ledge up to the cleft; yards a horse would travel faster than man. The logistics of it staggered Canada, and his spirits lowered.

Still, Crowbait was a horse with special training, and maybe that tedious time spent with the gelding would pay off now. Canada dreaded bringing the animal into the range of the killer's fire — and yet it was their only hope. He wasn't even sure the canny gelding would obey him under these circumstances, but he had to try.

He crawled back until he was safe under cover. He was frightened; his heart banged. He had never known such fear. He stood, flattening himself against the cliff.

"Crowbait!" he rasped. "Crowbait!" The

voice carried weakly out into the sun, but the animal heard, turned his head.

"Come, Crowbait. *Come!*" The gelding stood, not very willing.

"I said *Come!*" Canada barked. Languorously, the horse moved a few feet forward. The mare stood stock-still.

A screeching shot lashed the slope. Canada saw rock puff where it hit, well short of the horses.

"Linda," he said quietly. "If you can, aim your pistol through the crack where you can see the promontory. Make it count. Go slowly. Maybe one every thirty seconds to pin him down while the horses come in."

"I'll try," she whispered.

He heard her pull herself to her feet. She had no strength at all.

"Come, Crowbait!"

The old Colt bucked in Linda's double-handed grip. This time the horse moved forward, and the mare followed.

"Come! Turn left!" Canada barked. The horse looked down at him and ever so slowly turned leftward, staying high, beyond rifle range. Canada was elated. The gelding remembered.

A howling shot splattered the far slope but still below the horses. Linda saw movement and fired the Colt.

"Now right! Right, Crowbait!"

The horse turned slowly until it faced Canada. It was time for the run straight downslope.

"Okay, Linda. Crowbait will run in now. Pin that killer down. You've got four shots left. Better, use the rifle. There's a box of shells. Do you know how?"

She nodded, her emerald eyes blazing. "I practiced. I've been waiting for this moment a long time," she said darkly.

"Run, Crowbait! Run!" Canada roared.

She pressed the stock into her shoulder and fired; yanked the bolt and slammed another shell home, and fired, this time at something glinting up there. The flash of metal disappeared. She heard hooves scrambling downslope behind her. She fired again, this time into the roots of the gnarled pine up there, and something puffed up.

A screeching shot racketed down, hit nothing. She fired again, coldly, and saw sandstone spray. The hooves grew loud behind her and then stopped. Canada swiftly shoved the gelding into shadowed safety.

"Good boy," he said softly, scratching under the gelding's jaw.

The skittish mare stood agonizingly exposed beyond Canada's reach.

Linda fired again, and the terrified mare plunged backward — just as a wailing shot from above pierced the space where she had been. Canada dashed out and dragged her to safety.

He saddled deliberately and drew the cinches cautiously. Carelessness would destroy them now. Crowbait dragged the reata with him, and Canada rolled it up. Then he reloaded the two empty chambers of the old Colt with balls and powder from his saddlebag. He had no holster, so he wedged it into his belt.

"We'll run for it," he said tersely. "Toward that cleft up there. Hope it goes to cap rock."

"You don't know?"

"No. And getting there won't be a picnic. I'll cover with the pistol while you run. Then from there, you cover with the rifle while I run."

The moment had come. They stared tensely at each other, wondering if it was their last. Then he lifted her into the saddle and eased her numb, useless leg into the stirrup. The mare was unruly.

Canada positioned himself at the crack. Hooves rattled behind him; he heard her kicking and slapping. He fired carefully. There was a rattle on the slope behind.

Then a whining shot from above. The sound of scrambling hooves, the passage of life through the field of death. Canada fired again. And again. And then it was quiet. He peered back. She had made it. He could see her in the lee of the cleft, unsheathing the rifle, dismounting, tying up the mare, and easing down to an exposed corner where she could fire.

Canada fired his pistol one last time, leaped up on Crowbait, heart hammering, and touched the gelding's flanks. The horse plunged out into the naked sun, leaping up-slope, around boulders, across logs.

Canada heard shots. Saw dirt leap. Heard Linda's rifle bark. He kicked Crowbait hard. The gelding, unused to such treatment, veered sideways in a rotating movement as a shrieking bullet whipped under his belly. Uphill, all uphill. The horse gathered himself in leaps, plunged, and suddenly flew into the shadowed lee of the cleft.

She rose up, her eyes full of wetness. He jumped down and hugged her fiercely. They clung together, shaking like aspens in a breeze. Then he looked up the cleft, its slopes and ledges, and felt sick.

"We've got to do it. Got to. I'll want you on Crowbait, now. I'll lead him. I want that flatland mare unburdened."

She got on, and he led them up, gasping for breath. There was no walking in it. Only clambering over ledges, jumping up the rough stairwell. Crowbait gashed his hock. The mare opened a cut on her gaskin. Yet the spirited animals, perhaps sensing the urgency of it, never faltered, gathering, leaping, gathering again, sometimes negotiating five-foot ledges, higher than the corrals that contained them at home. They scraped their bellies, blood ran from pasterns and fetlocks. But they climbed like mountain goats.

Then, with victory in sight, Canada's heart sank. Before him was not another shelf but a giant fissure, perhaps ten feet across, with the upper lip feet above the lower, where he stood. There was rubble along one side, a six-inch wide lip where perhaps a human could cross. But not horses. He looked down into the fissure. There was no dipping in and out of it. He looked nervously back down the cleft. There was no one. He didn't expect anyone. The man on the promontory was ten or fifteen minutes from here.

He eased carefully around the fissure and up onto the cap rock. A huge coulee separated this place from the promontory; offered them time — if they could get the horses up. He returned, unsaddled the horses, and delicately carried the gear around the lip of the fissure. Then he helped Linda past the chasm until they both were up above.

He clenched his fists, stood fearfully across the chasm from the horse he loved. "Come," he said softly. "Come, old boy." The horse stood at the brink below, lifting one foot and then another, gathering and balking, restless and terrified.

"Come!" Canada cried, and the frightened animal plunged upward. His front hooves landed safely; his rear ones pummeled air, clawed at the vertical sandstone, scraped violently. Then he was there, above, with fresh red cuts across his rear legs. He walked to Canada and nickered and squealed and nuzzled the man who had asked from him his all.

"Okay," he barked to the mare, "your turn." The mare whinnied desperately, not wanting to be left behind. Then she solved the problem her own way, her Thoroughbred flatland way. She backed down the cleft to give herself a running start. Then bolted forward with a series of leaps, and then flew gracefully over the fissure, landing well beyond danger.

Pent up fear and breath exploded from Canada and Linda. Joyously they hugged the mare. Canada saddled once again. There was cap rock here stretching out as far as he could see. They would ride without leaving a trail, and could choose their exit from the cap rock. It would take days, maybe a week, for the man behind them to pick up the trail.

Cautiously, studying every rock in the direction of the promontory, they eased out into the open. They saw nothing. Then he lifted his beloved into her saddle and they rode down the sandstone ridge, down the wind, bleeding, wounded, still desperate, hungry, but alive.

CHAPTER FOURTEEN

He lifted her off the mare and carried her into the hideout cave. Fireball wasn't there. He lowered her gently onto her bedroll. He took care of the horses and their wounds and then dropped wearily beside Linda in the warm night.

He felt relatively safe for a day or two. He had stayed on the high rock, leaving no sign. They rode off the rock at a place artfully chosen, an unlikely passage into a carpet of needles, and farther away, out upon drying meadows. Yet, despite all that, he laid the rifle beside him, at the ready.

Linda was gaunt. Canada slipped off her boot and unwound the dressing from her swollen calf. The limb was infected and ugly with drainage. The dread thought of gangrene pinioned him. She stared at the mess, and then up at him. She knew.

"Would you marry someone with a leg cut off," she asked sadly, eyes glistening wetly.

"Would you marry someone with a hole in his chest, ditch in his skull, and brains scrambled with fear?" he replied.

He heated water until it bubbled and then washed Linda's wounds, flushing out the suppuration with water as hot as she could bear. Then he rummaged around in Fireball's gear for the whiskey he knew was there.

"Linda. Take this stick and hang on to it. Close your eyes. This is going to pretty near slay you."

He poured the hundred-proof stuff into the hole in her calf, and her whole body convulsed. Then he poured more into the exit hole, but she never cried, though her face was wet. Then he took clean bandage, soaked it in whiskey, and wrapped the calf once again.

She sank into a stupor while the fiery pain slowly subsided into the pulsing ache she had become familiar with.

He had work to do on himself: his hip was a bloodsoaked mess from the lead that had exploded off his holster. He bathed the area while she dozed, and picked fragments of metal out of his skin with his jackknife. His hipbone and the flesh around it were bruised and angry. He soaked the whole area in the fiery whiskey and then collapsed into fitful sleep.

He awoke suddenly a few hours later. The night was velvety and warm. He listened alertly, but the rhythms of the crickets were undisturbed. Restlessly he arose in the blackness. He could see the ghostlike bulk of the horses cropping grass in the sequestered park below. He listened some more, then surveyed the deeps of the darkness with his spyglass. There was nothing.

"What was it?" Linda asked, awake.

"My own fears," he replied shortly.

She sat up, hearing something troubled in his voice.

"I don't want to die, either," she said. "I'm sick of this — this running, and fear, and blood."

"Want to go back East?"

"I thought you'd ask," she replied bitterly. "You don't really believe."

"Believe what?"

"Believe that I'm real! That I love you! That this is my home and Montana is where I'll live, and die, and have children —"

"Whose?" he said curtly.

She stared quietly up at him, not daring to say what she needed to say, sensing he would somehow twist it and stamp on it. Something hung in balance just then. One wrong word, she knew, would destroy all that had been built. She remembered, then, the sadness she had first seen in him, and his transformation that March morning out among his horses.

"It must be unbearable to you, losing all the horses you love, except Crowbait," she said tenderly, with some sad melody in her voice.

"They're all I had. Most like a family, I guess, only I never had one. . . . Never had a wife, never had kids, my flesh and blood, to raise up, or talk to. Those horses were all."

"They *were* your family," she whispered. "And you never let me see you grieving for them, not even when you didn't know whether you'd ever see them again. It was like burying your father and mother again, out on the prairie, and just walking away, all empty, and only half grown-up."

She saw an agony upon his features, visible even in the starlight, a loneliness so terrible, so deep, so haunting that it was beyond burying, or growing out of, or putting into the past. She reached up to slip her hand into his work-hastened rough one, and she pulled him down beside her.

"Tell me your dream," she whispered.

"Haven't any now."

"Yes you do, Canada Parker!" She laughed

unexpectedly, not giving him any sympathy at all. She wanted him to think of the future — their future.

He grinned. Couldn't help it with that joy pealing out of the glorious girl beside him.

He knew she understood. But she wasn't letting him sink into self-pity once again. She was inviting him to put his loneliness and need forever behind him. To step away from it. To grow.

"Well, I reckon I'd like about three good studs, and forty, fifty blooded mares, and a mess of Thoroughbreds, and a bunch of quarter horses, though their blood's all mixed up."

"And?"

"And some good blooded cattle, Herefords look mighty nice. A dog, any old friendly mutt. Some cats in the barn. Few ornery chickens. A hog for the slop."

"Is that all?"

"All! Ain't that enough?" He glared at her, and she glared back.

She laughed huskily, unmistakably.

"You're always upsettin' my sense of propriety," he bellowed.

He jumped up and began a strange ritual. He soaped his stubbled chin and scraped it clean with his battered straightedge. Then he stripped off his flannel shirt and scrubbed furiously. Then he buttoned up again and sat cross-legged before her in the velvet dark.

He cleared his throat. "If you'd have me, I'd like to . . . I mean, you're more than a man could want. Have a family. Rowdy redheaded boys. Little girls with pony-tails . . ."

"Yes."

"Yes what?"

"Yes, I'll marry you, you idiot. I've been trying to say so for days!" She ran a hand tenderly along his smooth cheek. "Now we've just got to stay alive . . ."

A somberness settled upon them as they thought about the perils ahead. Two targeted people in hills full of deadly men. They sat quietly and watched the dawn break.

"I'd like to get to the McFarlands as soon as we are strong enough," she said. "We'll be safe there. The VP isn't worth this — this death everywhere. No property is worth that. I just want you, and life, and any future we can fashion, even if we start out with nothing."

He sat pensively, absorbing that. "Running away? We're not cowards, Linda. Like some whipped dogs?"

"Canada, it isn't cowardice! It's death and loss and terror to stay here in the mountains.

There's just two of us, and an army of them."

"I'd like to get my horses back . . ."

"Of course! I want my things back too! But I want you more. I don't want you to throw away your life, or mine, for your horses," she said urgently.

He sighed, seeing the sense of her ideas yet wanting to fight the outlaws until the hills were free of them and a man could live in peace.

"Canada, your friend Fireball is organizing a force of cattlemen and lawmen to do the job. It's not our job. I've never shot at a human being in my life until now! Neither have you! We did, in self-defense, but you and I aren't — I mean, let the trained ones do it."

"I'm no better with arms than most of those cattlemen who have got up the courage to go after these hardcases," Canada said. "I'm no different. We've all got to risk gettin' hurt."

She squeezed his hand, liking his manhood even though she didn't understand it all.

"Well, if you must, join them when they come. You'll have a chance to live, at least . . ." she said somberly. The talk died then, with nothing settled.

"Canada," she said at long last, "you bring new life into the world. Foals, colts, and fillies that are beautiful. And later you train them to be useful creatures. That's walking beside God, I think. Bringing up new life and making it useful. That's what I want to do, too. I want . . . our babies, yours and mine. And I want them to be strong and upright, that's what I'll teach them. And . . . Canada, I'm terrified for us!"

She threw her arms around him and hugged him hungrily. He held her a long time, knowing at last that they had to get out of the Bulls for the sake of their dream, knowing that her wounded leg required attention and immobilized them anyway, jeopardizing them anywhere they went in these mountains.

"We'll go, honey," he murmured. "We'll get down to Stuart's and have Anne start doctorin' your leg."

"Tomorrow?"

"Tonight probably, if you're up to it. And the horses. Crowbait's pretty skinned up."

The tension that had knotted her released, and she curled up in her bedroll and slept a restful sleep. Canada watched her, loving the serenity on her face in repose, and the tawny tangle of her hair. Then he dozed beside her in the morning sun. The healing

271

sleep deepened in them. Their exhausted bodies and minds slipped into a long oblivion.

It was in the midst of this vast unrolling deep that he heard Crowbait whinnying. It came again, urgently, this horse-talk with a message for his master. It penetrated slowly through the blanketed layers of weariness, until finally, when Canada opened his eyes in the afternoon sun, he heard nothing at all. A dread rose in him. He shook away the last shreds of slumber and started down upon the sequestered glade. It was empty. The horses were gone.

"Crowbait!" he cried into the emptiness, to the horse that had been almost brother and son. "Crowbait!"

Linda stood beside him, drawn out of her own slumber by the desolation she felt lowering upon the one she loved. She understood.

"I've got to get him. I've got to follow," he cried desperately.

"I'm coming with you," she said.

"But, Linda. Your leg. You can't. You'll slow us down. I plan to move fast. I've got to catch up!"

"I'm coming! My leg isn't broken. It's only pain I have to worry about."

He saw something fierce in her that would

not brook resistance.

"If I stay here, I'll never see you alive again," she said dully, and he knew somehow that some woman's intuition was speaking to her.

"I've learned to accept pain. Then it becomes bearable. I learned that not long ago," she smiled.

He raced to the cave for a canteen, jerky, lariat, and his pistol.

"We're goin' light. Weight would slow us down," he said, plunging down the gravelly slope to the meadow. She lunged after him, gimping along on a howling leg, gritting hard against the waves of ache that pulsed up.

"Someone came in from the south, from the VP," Canada said, studying tracks. "He roped Crowbait; here's where he resisted and jerked. That's the only way to take him. He won't stand for much handlin' by strangers."

They walked north, following a clear fresh trail of three shod horses. Whoever took them was probably not the manhunter, Canada reasoned. This had to be a chance encounter, a theft, probably by one of the hardcases who had an eye for profit and no loyalty at all to his employer.

Canada raced ahead on long legs and

Linda gamely followed, her face gray with pain. It was the way to Roundup, not Mc-Farland's, but it no longer mattered. She felt the little derringer in her coat pocket thump against her as she walked, and she felt comforted by it.

The thief had followed the broad valleys, not bothering at all to conceal his trail northward, for who was there to object to a hardcase collecting some strays, especially that fine-looking mare?

Canada stopped to stare despairingly at the prints. Some were drying, a tiny rim of white dust forming around their periphery.

"He's gaining on us, getting ahead," Canada gritted. Neither of them paid much attention to their continuing exposure, their naked walk down the center of the valleys.

He stopped at last under a ponderosa and handed the canteen to Linda. She was gray; the flesh of her face had drawn taut and there were rims of blackness under her eyes. He was horrified, wishing she had stayed in the safety of the cave where she could heal.

She saw his glare and smiled. "I haven't slowed you yet, Canada Parker. I have a free will, just as you do, and I elect to stay with you if I can."

The sheer grit of it, if not impertinence, suddenly warmed him.

"I don't know who I love most, Crowbait or you," he grinned malevolently. "Crowbait, I think."

"Crowbait doesn't kiss," she said softly.

"No, but he's obedient," Canada retorted, smiling.

They strode onward again, covering perhaps three miles in the next hour. Linda never complained, kept his pace, and made her wounded leg follow the rhythm of his steps. They passed through a valley dotted with 30-Mile cattle, and another full of Ezekiel Earley's stock.

"The Sanders place is yonder to the east," Canada explained. "And still full of hijacked cattle."

He stopped at last in twilight and stared at the game girl beside him. "Do you realize, Mrs. Van Pelt, that you've walked over ten miles with a bullet hole in your leg? We're farther north now than that box canyon where we had the fight. Maybe four to Roundup."

"I don't feel anything any more. It's numb," she said.

"We'll be in Roundup before midnight," he said.

"You're not going to stop?"

He looked at her sadly, knowing her ordeal.

"I can't see the tracks any more. But they're going to Roundup and that's my only chance to get Crowbait and the mare."

"I'm good for ten more," she grinned. "Call it love, if you really want to know."

The words — or the young woman's gallantry — put something in Canada's heart that had never been there before. It had no name, for on the one hand it was a tender reverence for her, almost awe, and on the other, he felt orphaned no more; he knew at last he was loved.

"See the North Star ahead of us. That's what you are to me, that's the way my compass is always pointin'."

She smiled in the dark.

They struck the Musselshell River well east of the settlement, and that suited them. Far to the left across the bottoms they could see lights hard by the river.

"I don't want you gettin' that wound wet," he said, pulling off his boots. He lifted her bodily and carried her across the shallows.

"We're just going to have to hunt from one end of town to the other, and stay concealed doing it. Those who aren't hardcases here are hard men, likely to shoot. If we find Crowbait, we'll just have to do a little pilferin' of our own."

They worked warily up the east side of

the settlement. The horses were not at the saloon hitch rail nor in the corrals out back. Canada whistled softly to the dark bulk of horses there beside the bunkhouse, but there was no answering nicker. They walked north, probing several other frame or log buildings. They filtered softly among them, first on one side of the road, then the other. Dark discouragement mounted in Canada. He began to grieve.

The horses simply weren't in Roundup.

"I'm very tired and I'm hungry," Linda said, feeling as low as he did.

"The saloon's still open — only it's not a place for ladies. Maybe I can rustle up some chow there if the kitchen's not closed. I'll bring it out."

It didn't matter to her how he did it. She just wanted to collapse awhile. There was a covered freight wagon, she remembered, in the rear of Grizzly Bear's yard. She could rest there.

It looked pretty good to Canada. The back of the wagon, with the tailgate down, opened out on the river. She could slip away safely if she had to. He helped her in and watched her curl up instantly on the plank bed.

The saloon was nearly empty, and Grizzly Bear was counting the night's proceeds. One poker game was still in progress; a loner, a hardcase Canada had seen, drank alone, covered with trail dust.

"We're closing up, pilgrim. You'll have one drink," Polarski announced, filling a glass.

"Is the kitchen open? That's what I wanted."

"No it ain't," Polarski said. "Fat's all folded up."

"I'd like to buy grub — anything."

"Tomorrow, pilgrim. Drink up now."

The Chinese swamper drew close, frankly staring at Canada, while Polarski returned to his tallying.

"Return in half an hour," whispered the Celestial. "Food and news."

"What?" Canada asked, puzzled.

"You heard." The man swabbed the bar with a rag and vanished.

Canada sucked the rotgut and eyed the hardcase narrowly. He could be the one.

"Closing time, gents," Polarski bellowed, blowing out lamps.

Canada drifted out when the loner did. The man unhitched a strange horse and led it to the corral in back. Then he disappeared into the bunkhouse.

The poker players walked uptown. Then Polarski left, abandoning the saloon to the swamper. Canada checked on Linda and found her asleep. He tarried at the river, then softly approached the door with his pistol drawn. He didn't know, really, what to expect. Death, perhaps.

"Good evening Mr. Parker," said the middle-aged Chinese.

"You know my name."

"Is Mrs. Van Pelt with you? Or Mr. Reed?"

Canada was startled. "What business is it of yours?" he rasped.

"My humble pardon," Fat Son Lee grinned. "Mr. Reed employs me, along with Mr. Bell of the NP. I am Fat Son Lee, an agent of Pinkerton's."

Canada stared narrowly, absorbing that. Then grinned.

"We have no word of Mrs. Van Pelt or James Reed. It is most urgent. Mr. Bell asked also for news of you."

Canada sighed, running a hand through his unkempt hair, still not quite trusting. Fat Son Lee waited patiently, missing nothing.

"You are on foot," he said suddenly.

"Now how would you know that?"

"Detectives, Mr. Parker, are trained to be observant. Your pants are wet to the knee, and I have made a deduction. . . . Now come along, there's a meal ready."

"I need food for two. Is it safe for me to be here?"

"Relatively. You will eat in the kitchen and there is a rear door. The front is now barred."

Canada sank wearily into a kitchen chair.

"Reed is dead. Bushwacked. Linda's with me. My horse — my — you wouldn't understand that, about the horse — is stolen and her mare. Linda was shot in the leg. I don't know how she walks, but she does."

"Please get her immediately," the Chinese said gravely. "Where is she?"

"Out in the wagon yonder."

Fat opened the door and Canada, feeling the urgency of his request, slipped into the blackness and carried her, sleeping, into the kitchen.

"On the table, please," Fat insisted.

Canada hesitated.

"I'm a physician and surgeon. In fact it was my humble but sad task to treat your wound in your chest and arrange your delivery to McFarland's."

Light burst in Canada. He was seeing the man who had saved his life, the man unknown who had transported him that night from the road somewhere. . . . Canada swallowed hard, quite without words.

Fat Son Lee, M.D., was already at work unwinding the bandage under the orange glow of the kerosene lamp. He stared a long time at the wound, the entrance and exit holes.

"I am very impressed, Mr. Parker."

"You're talkin' in riddles."

"I had expected infection, perhaps gangrene. A lot of swelling. Suppuration. An area bearing the blue and purple of violent impact. But look for yourself . . ."

Canada realized that the leg was vastly better now, even after fifteen miles of hiking.

"The long walk brought fresh blood to the area, apparently, to reduce the inflammation. That's the only explanation I have. The poisons were drawn off by that constant pumping of her muscles. But she could not have walked with such a wound without conquering pain. Willing herself to ignore it. My congratulations, Mr. Parker."

"You're still talkin' riddles."

"She loves you a great deal. Only love would enable someone with pain of that magnitude to walk with you."

Canada laughed. "I don't know whether you're doctorin' or detectin'."

Linda smiled, awake. "He loves Crowbait more than he loves me," she said softly.

"Ah, Mrs. Van Pelt. I grieve at the news of your father," Fat said, bandaging her calf once more.

She sighed. "His last words were, 'Get Fat.' I didn't understand them . . ."

The Chinese motioned for her to eat, and set thick soup before them.

"You are missing treasured horses," Fat said. "The gentleman who arrived before you; the one you saw, perhaps. He did come from the north."

"North? He's not the one, then," Canada said gloomily.

"I beg your pardon. When one comes from the south with horses he wishes to conceal from other eyes here at this unique saloon with its unique clientele, he's likely to put them in the livery at the stage stop at the north end of town, safely hidden in box stalls, and then ride back here."

Canada's heart missed a beat.

"Crowbait's here! There?"

"Merely hypothesis," the swamper said. "If you'll permit me, I shall mop a little and examine the front windows for prying eyes."

They spooned their broth gratefully, filling empty caverns within.

The Oriental returned and sat himself at the table. The swamper had somehow vanished in him, and Canada found himself eyeing a cool operative.

"Now then, Mr. Parker. Certain parties could use all information you can divulge.

In short, you may be able to save lives if you would. Not to mention breaking this ring, restoring your horses to you, and stolen stock to the rest."

Canada told his story, then, as best he could, wishing all the while he could rescue Crowbait.

"That's valuable," Fat said at last. "We didn't know, for example, that the ring had moved down to the VP or that the Sanders are dead. Their death was anticipated, but couldn't be helped."

"Who are *we*?" Canada asked irritably.

"The Cattlemen's Protective Association and your colleague, Fireball Fenton. They will be here shortly, perhaps tomorrow. The plan had been to overmaster as many as possible here at the saloon at night, and then circle the Sanders ranch in the small hours later. Now we shall change it."

"How are you gettin' information out?"

"The stages three times a week. And a colleague of mine, a certain coal miner, when necessary. This is confidential of course. Not a soul knows who I am other than Mr. Bell. And not even he knows the name of my colleague, the miner. None of the cattlemen know who I am. Now, then, what are your plans?"

"Get the horses," Canada replied tersely.

"You know, in a settlement like this the livery is guarded at night. We shall have to devise a strategy. And where will you go then? Surely not back south."

Canada rubbed his head wearily. He hadn't given any thought to it.

"I just train horses," he said dully.

"And very well, I understand," Fat said gently. "There's no safe place for you in this camp. I would suggest you head west, up the Musselshell. The cattlemen's vigilante force will be coming that way."

"Can you stand a couple more hours?" Canada asked Linda.

"More if I must."

"Now then, the livery. My own horse is there, and they are used to my coming and going at odd hours. Orientals are . . . inscrutable, you know," he smiled. "I'll need a way to identify yours if they are there. And I must remind you, you'll have no saddles or bridles. I can lend you bridles."

While he talked he loaded a gunnysack with provisions.

"Grizzly owes you this grub. He didn't give you the proper change for your double eagle that night."

"You saw that?" Canada asked, astonished.

"Operatives must be observant," Fat

smiled. "Come along. You two are about to rent horses."

"In the middle of the night?"

"It is not uncommon here," Fat replied. "But let me talk. Follow your clues, listen well."

When they arrived the little livery office was empty, though the lamp burned.

"We're in luck. I was hoping for as much. The gentleman gets bored and goes for little strolls on occasion. Find your horses in the dark, please."

"Crowbait," Canada called softly. A loud nicker to the left. Canada joyously opened the stall. Next to it, in the blackness, he found a mare. He hoped it was the right one, for he had only his hands for guides. The Chinese handed him the bridles.

"Quickly now. I hear him, I believe, and I shall have to go complain about my mare's lameness. Good luck!"

Canada reached out in the dark and found a hand and grasped it with some upwelling warmth and gratitude. And then the man was gone.

He boosted Linda up and they slipped out into the black, moving swiftly through shadowed lanes, past log and frame buildings where hard men and hard women slept, and finally to the gurgling river.

They turned west, in starlight.

And just half a mile ahead of them was the man called Yuma.

CHAPTER FIFTEEN

There were tears blurring Yuma's eyes. The last shot from below had smashed into sandstone just inches from his face, exploding rock into a thousand fiery darts that jabbed into his right eye, his cheek, ear, and forehead.

It was his aiming eye, the one he used so well to favor people. Now it ran wet and swelled shut, and the other eye ran, too. The shots from below continued, but he could do nothing except fire blindly while Parker and the girl made good their escape.

Some vast irritation boiled up in him, fracturing his normal calm. What had he taken on a woman-hunt for? Things had gone wrong. They *never* had gone wrong before. He thought he had them up here. Their flank was exposed. It had been a classical enfilade, the sort described in the military texts.

He washed his face and eye with canteen

water and finally freed the open one of blurry tears. It would have to do.

He sulked down to his horse, far below in the bottoms of the box canyon, and then rode it back up to the cleft where his quarry had vanished. Yuma worked painfully to the top, only to discover the fissure blocking all progress. So! He would have had them trapped in here if he hadn't have been blinded! But there were no downward hoof-prints. Nothing leading away from the cleft. He climbed to the cap rock on top and found nothing at all. No horse could jump that fissure, nor could man induce a horse to try.

He searched for sign the whole next day and then retreated gloomily toward the VP. He hadn't fulfilled his contract with Preacher so he had no claim on half. Worse, if Parker and the girl got out of the Bulls safely, they would scarcely remain silent. No one ever had been able to accuse him of anything. Until now.

Yuma rode uneasily south, churning over the somber realities. The more he traveled, the more reluctant he was to face Preacher. He could do the favor to Preacher easily from ambush. But he couldn't run the VP. Preacher's spellbinding held those men there. And he would inherit none of the things he had hoped for if that horse trainer reached safety. Only posses, vigilantes, and the law.

The more Yuma pondered it, the less sure he was that he wanted to go back to the VP. In fact, some old officer's instinct told him to cut and run; he was a marked man, in a death trap that would break the rustling ring brutally, and stretch plenty of necks.

He cursed. He had never done the favor to a woman before. He knew better. How did Preacher ever rope him into it? From the first, he had seen trouble. He had been fired on. His victims could identify him.

He wished he could get something out of it. That black stallion at the VP for instance. All he had to do was slip in at night, or broad daylight for that matter, and take it. Who'd suspect? Small enough reward for his hard, lonely life. Portable. It would trot right along with him to the gold camps, Maiden or Gilt Edge, or maybe down to Virginia City or Bannock.

He could run the horse in match races and clean up on wagers. Mine the miners. Retire that British rifle for a while until things cooled down. Sell stud fees. Brand the sonofabitch with his own mark. That was horseflesh of a sort rarely seen in this country. Kentucky stuff. Something that would whip the best those Butte copper kings had.

Trouble was, the VP was heavily guarded. A man would likely have the favor done him if he rode in there at night. . . . He'd just have to do it by day, lie a little to old Preacher and walk out with the stud. Yuma grinned and spurred his mount into an easy lope.

He found Preacher over at the corrals where some artists with running irons were at work on some calves. Yuma rode up to the thin gray man; he liked looking down from the saddle.

"There's been a chimney fire at Pike and Maudie's," he said softly. "Too bad they were just a mite careless. I didn't see signs of life, nor even their poor old remains," he announced woefully.

Preacher gazed sideways and up and down. "Lord took 'em off," he sighed. "Nice respectable folk."

"They had guests."

"Guests, you say?"

"Parker. Mrs. Van Pelt."

Preacher frowned, lifted his battered hat and ran a hand through his gray-streaked hair.

"And this fire — ?"

"Yup. Sad it was, snuffing out the young.

But it was a favor to 'em, him so full of pain and her . . ."

Some black antagonism flared in Preacher's face and for a moment Yuma thought the man would favor him. But the moment dissolved. Yuma decided it was not the time to turn his back. The man before him was one spasm of the trigger finger away from sole mastery of the Bulls.

The fifty-fifty deal means nothing to him, Yuma realized. *I'll get out fast.*

"I'll wash up and chow down at the big house, partner," he said casually, dropping the "sir" forever.

He slid off the horse easily, but used the animal for cover all the while. The sleek black stallion was still in its pen, trotting restlessly. It would be easy at the nooning.

Yuma unsaddled and walked his jaded mount into the corrals. He'd need a fresh beast, a good one, for the escape. One with bottom, one that would outstay followers.

"Brother Yuma, hold a moment."

The sepulchered voice of Preacher startled the bantam officer. Preacher was there beside him, sending prickles up Yuma's spine. A bushwacker Yuma might be, but no match for Preacher's draw.

"Brother Yuma, why are you lying to me? I plain know you're lying. I hear voices roll-

291

ing down from heaven above, and one told me clear as day that my trusted partner is lying."

The words of the gaunt man staggered Yuma, and he stammered.

"Sir, you're . . . just . . . imagining . . ."

"No! I'm not! Yuma, how could you do this? Parker's alive, and so is the woman."

The quiver in Yuma's voice betrayed him.

"Preacher, sir . . ."

"You'll be consigned to hell, Yuma, for holdin' back from me."

It was an eerie thing. But Preacher was just bluffing, Yuma figured. Had to be.

"Care to ride over to Sanders for a look?" he said cockily.

"Hell and eternal damnation," Preacher thundered. "A traitor in my bosom."

Yuma broke into cold sweat. Some ancient sentence from a military text came to mind, one he had adopted as a motto: Audacity will carry the day sometimes where even calculated force would fail.

Yuma glanced around the yard. The branding crew had dispersed for chow. They were alone.

"We can settle this easy." He grinned. "You believe in signs and all that. I'll flip a coin. Heads I'm telling the gospel truth; tails I'm not."

The sheer confidence of it hung in the air. Yuma thought it might work either way. He'd have the drop on Preacher, looking down at the coin in the dust.

"Faithful men need no signs," Preacher boomed. "But for your sake, Brother Yuma, I'll consent to the test."

The coin flipped slowly into the blue, and arced lazily down into the yellow gumbo of the corral. Preacher bent low.

"Heads," he said, straightening up.

Yuma's hand slid the half-drawn pistol back.

"See now, you've got some apologizing to do, partner," Yuma said cheerfully.

A vast frown furrowed Preacher's face. Yuma walked casually with his back exposed to the big log house, washed up, and entered, still feeling Preacher's odd gaze upon him.

From then on it was easy. He devoured a bowl of beans, repacked his saddlebags, threw his saddle over a fine steeldust with a fresh Bar OB Bar brand. Preacher stood at the corral rail, not seeing anything in particular. Yuma haltered the glossy black stallion and took off.

"See you, partner," he said as he trotted past the bemused man. He rode easily up the long slope until he could look down upon the solid VP. Far below, Preacher still stood mutely at the corrals, in a strange reverie that Yuma couldn't understand.

"Should have done you the big favor, Preacher my friend," he said, grinning broadly as he trotted over the crest of the ridge and out upon a wilderness of rock and forest and meadow. North to the Musselshell, then west. The Big Snowies first, high country to rest up in. Then Lewistown and the quartz-gold camp up at Maiden. He heard it was booming day and night.

"Sorry, partner," he guffawed.

Linda weaved on the mare, clinging mutely to her mane. Canada wasn't much better off, but he was determined to put some miles between Roundup and themselves before they dared to rest. It was perhaps three in the morning and the summer dawn was not far off. The river bubbled peacefully beside them. The bottoms were usually easy to travel, level, with plenty of feed and water. The only trouble with rivers was that other people used them for highways too.

Later, Crowbait stopped, ears perked forward. Canada touched the gelding's flanks but it moved forward only one step.

"Okay, boy," Canada breathed. It was a signal Canada knew, one he had drilled into the animal a thousand times.

"Indians, is it?"

The horse was named Crowbait for a reason, Canada thought grimly. The Crows were masterful horse thieves and not infrequently raided Canada's horse ranch in the nearby Bulls.

He slid off the big gelding, taking care to land with a feathery silence. He nudged Linda, who came awake instantly from her stupor.

The moon was down. The river was close, laughing through the gloom. Sandstone cliffs loomed close across the water, but were distant on their side. He could see nothing, yet he felt the presence of menace alive in the night.

He lifted Linda off the mare just as a horse somewhere ahead whinnied. The mare exploded into life, whinnying, nickering, pawing in the dark. Canada was astonished. It was the neighing of old friends and yet the mare had none here. Or did she?

Ahead there was a faint rustle, then silence. Uncertainly, Canada considered retreat, but it was too late. They were in the middle of something. Canada slipped the bridle off Crowbait. He wanted no hands reaching out in the night to steal that horse. And in any case, it was the first step of a certain maneuver that he had drilled into Crowbait as a defense against Indians in the night . . .

But it was too late.

"Don't move," said a silken voice. "Now hands over your heads." The bulk of a small man was barely visible beside a Cottonwood.

Linda reached slowly into the pocket where her derringer still rested.

"Your hands too," said the soft commanding voice. "I do believe you are a woman, or else the starlight twists the shadows."

Linda hesitated.

"Lift them or die," snapped the voice.

The small man sifted closer and recognition iced through Linda.

"Why, if it isn't the horse trainer and Mrs. Van Pelt. My day is complete," the voice said softly. "And that nice mare, a fitting companion for my noble stallion."

Understanding washed through Canada. He saw blue steel in the night.

"At last!" breathed the bantam shadow. "A favor. Two favors. True reward. My luck doubles. Yours runs out."

"Why us?" Canada asked tightly.

"Because you have seen me. No one else ever did. And because you were my only failure. And you, madam, have aroused my curiosity. Now I shall satisfy myself." He laughed quietly.

It was now or never, Canada guessed.

"Indians, Crowbait. *Indians.*" The horse's ears rotated back to his master. It was a command, but one long unheard. He hesitated, then moved. Then the gelding plunged at Yuma.

"Hey!" the shadow bellowed. Then, *"Hey!"* The shadowy man dodged, fired wildly up at the horse.

The gelding whirled. Two powerful hind legs slashed out. Two shod hooves, knife-edged, slammed into the man's chest, catapulting him like a feather, back, back, and down into the stream. The hooves flew again. One brained the black-bearded man. Skull caved in. A finger convulsed. A crack; a geyser of water. Another crack. A whine in the night. A splash, rippling the river. A woman's scream. The horse reared, a thousand pounds whistling down upon two front hooves. A thud upon the spasming body half in water. Then quiet.

"The horse — it could do that?" whispered Linda.

"Crowbait's his name," Canada muttered shakily. He felt sick.

Yuma's body swirled free and drifted away, toward outlaw Roundup.

They sat down, too paralyzed to think. A whinny a hundred yards off. Wearily they walked through brush. The black stallion gleamed in the stars, and the steeldust nickered welcome.

"They're ours," Canada said joyously.

"That's the stallion. The one we brought you a century ago," Linda whispered.

Sleek and highbellied in the night. Canada slipped a powerful arm around Linda's waist as they watched him dance on his tether.

There was a small saddle, a roll, and gear.

"I don't want to stay here," Linda said, shuddering

They saddled the steeldust, loaded up, and trudged west. Canada led them up and out of the bottoms, away from the traffic of the night, far onto the rolling prairie, and finally to a rock-guarded swale beside some stunted pines.

"We didn't know his name," she whispered.

"His name was Darkness," Canada replied.

"He killed my father," she said flatly.

"Don't think about it any more."

"I can't help it," she wept. "Oh, God."

He rolled out the blankets and she collapsed into them. He rigged a picket line, and staked the stallion apart.

In the dark he found Crowbait and hugged him, hoping she didn't see. Hugged the big muzzling blunderbuss of a horse until the crystal stars were white blurs. Then he collapsed beside her unconscious form, even as the gray of false dawn kissed the east. . . .

The sun was high. There was a face beside his, and a woman's arm across him. And a slim, angular body pressed to him, close, needing and giving even in sleep. He brushed a wisp of red hair from a tearstained face and kissed those closed eyes until they opened like great emeralds in the sun.

"Where are we going today?" she asked.

"Home."

"Aren't they still there? — the hardcases?"

"Home is where the heart is," he grinned. "Where's yours?"

"In a bathtub."

He stared slantwise at her. "I've got you headed but not heeled," he said at last.

"What does that mean?"

"Means I'm not home yet."

"I give up!" she said, throwing off her blankets.

It was high noon when they broke camp. Back down in the bottoms, they cut a trail.

"Lot of 'em went through last night,"

Canada said contemplatively. "Heading for Roundup. Shod, all of them. At least a dozen, maybe twice that."

"The cattlemen?"

"Could be," he said. "We can keep wandering west or we can go find out."

"Back into danger?"

"Could be."

They turned east. Linda thought she would know where they brushed death, but it was all different by daylight.

Canada drew up in a nest of cottonwoods west of town, and led the horses into the intimate shade.

"I'll go scout, Linda. You stay out of sight now. You've still got that hideout gun?"

"Yes."

He left her to watch the flies of summer plague the horses. She slid down to the river and splashed water over her face. Delightful! She slipped out of her shirtwaist and scrubbed furiously, stripping away grit and dirt and dust and saddle gum. When she returned to the copse the whole world glowed clean. She was happy.

The ravaged look on Canada's face when he returned stunned her. He wore an expression she had never seen.

"They were here," he said shortly.

"Can we go into town, then?"

"No!"

She stared at him, dreading whatever he was about to say.

"There were some hangings. Seven of 'em. Vigilante justice is a little careless."

He sat gloomily on a log, twisting his hat in his hands, trying to find some way of telling her.

"Canada, were there some —"

"Four were hardcases, three weren't."

"Three were innocent?" she gasped.

"Grizzly Bear. He wasn't part of it. And one I don't know, just passing through . . ."

"Yes?"

"And Fat!" he cried. The word hung ghastly in the air. Some force smashed Linda's stomach.

"Hung for fun. Threw in a Celestial." Canada spat.

"Oh, Canada," she breathed.

"He saved both our lives, and now —"

"Didn't they know who he was, didn't they —"

"No. No one knew. And even if they did . . . they might have . . . mobs are funny."

"I hate your West!" she cried. "Hate it. Hate it!"

"Not the land. The land's innocent."

"I hate it all," she cried. "Barbarian place!" She sat down on the log and sobbed.

"There's no difference between the badmen and the rest," she said bitterly.

She sat rigidly for long minutes, weeping for her father, for her husband, and for the quiet Oriental to whom they owed so much. Then, with a shudder, she looked up at Canada, and it was the look of a stranger.

"I'd like to go to Billings," she said quietly. "I belong in New York. My mother will need comforting. It was my fault, really, bringing my father here. We have a private car there to take me back. . . . I don't need anything from the VP. I'll sell it, give it away. I don't care."

He gazed at her, some pain welling up in him so terrible that he couldn't breathe.

"And us?" he choked.

She placed a hand gently over his. "I'll always love you in a special way," she said sadly.

"Then why —"

She sighed from some inner depth of pain.

"Because I don't belong here. It takes more than love. . . . Your world here is something I can't comprehend. Cruelty. Menace. Death."

"Is that what you see in me?" he asked bitterly.

"No, no, Canada."

"Don't you know I love you?" he said

302

savagely. "When people love each other can't they —"

She stood, facing him with a resignation on her face he couldn't grasp. She was surrendering to the foreordained.

"I'm a Reed," she said sternly. "I'm my father's daughter. The East won't be any better. It's a limbo now. The tiresome city or the savage West. I believe I will run my father's businesses now."

She sighed and lifted his hand to her lips a moment.

"Let's go, please. I'll risk whatever danger there may be on the stagecoach road."

Some inexpressible desolation settled over him as he gathered the animals together. Sadly, he forded the river there, away from town and its dangling horrors. They struck the stage road a little south; perhaps they could make it to McFarland's by early evening if they pressed.

They plodded down an empty, rutted road, he bareback, she upon a murderer's saddle. Two stunning horses came along behind. His mind was far away, remembering her first smiles in the cap-rock niche, kisses in the dark, hugs promising joys to come. Hints of things beyond all imagination. The sudden filling of his orphaned heart, love without fear of loss. Love eternal.

Love enduring, that wouldn't die and be buried on the prairies. Love persevering down the long halls of life.

He shuddered and Linda watched him sadly. She knew she had awakened something in his lonely heart, given him something precious only to take it away now. Still, there would be something left. Canada would have new strength, new courage, even alone.

The afternoon stretched out behind them. They saw and heard nothing, though they knew that somewhere to the east the same army of vigilantes were upon the pineclad slopes of Linda's ranch with death in their bellies.

Canada had withdrawn into himself so she made it her burden to watch, to stay alert. No shots. Nothing disturbed the day. No crows burst into flight. It was an empty land, matching the emptiness of her heart. Some day, after civilization had tamed this place, she would come back. But not now. Not just eight years after George Custer had met his doom not far away.

They rested once and then plodded on into shadows and finally night. Neither was hungry. Canada was so silent, so unaware of the world about him that she began an aimless chatter. But his desolation was stronger and it soon overpowered her soft talk. She loved him, and sorrowed.

They rode at last into the 30-Mile with the last twilight rimming the northern hills. Lamplight glowed warmly through windows. People, friendly people, emerged into the lavender night at the sound of horses.

She saw Stuart McFarland, and Anne, and recognized Mr. Bell.

"Canada," Anne moaned, sensing some terrible thing in him.

"We've been worried; desperate —" said Bell, reaching up to Linda. "Let me help you."

"I should have known you'd make it," Stuart said, trying for a note of cheer that failed. He gave up, led the horses to the pens, mildly curious about the Thoroughbreds.

"Dad's dead, Mr. Bell," Linda said.

"That's what the agent told us," he sighed. "Fat sent his man down here. We guessed you'd get here eventually."

"Fat Son Lee is dead," she whispered.

"Dead!"

"Hanged," she sobbed. "They didn't even wait to find out who he was . . ."

"Oh my God," Bell breathed, and collapsed heavily on the veranda steps. Of course they wouldn't have known. No one but himself knew.

"Damn vigilante mobs! Damn those stupid cattlemen. Half of them aren't any better than the ones they — I'm sorry, Mrs. Van Pelt. Terribly sorry."

"I want to go home now," she said. "To our car. It's still there, isn't it? And East. I must see my mother."

"Of course."

"Now?"

He paused. "I don't see why not. I have the buckboard. . . . You're limping."

"I was shot."

"Shot! Do you know by whom?"

"He's dead." Her face was something he didn't like to see.

"Come in, Canada, damn you," grumbled Anne. "I'll feed you both."

"You can tell me everything in the buckboard — if you would, Mrs. Van Pelt. We've a long drive."

"Where are — what's happening at my ranch?"

"We don't know yet."

"Can our car be coupled to the morning eastbound?"

"Yes, if we leave now and get you there in time. Is that wound — are you — how serious is it?"

"I can live with it. I have been, for as long

as I can remember. It's through my calf."

"Through?" he said, amazed. "Stuart, we've got to get her on the eastbound. I'll need the wagon harnessed, and my grays . . ."

It was done, then, while Linda and Canada sat mutely, she dreading the pain of parting; he already parted from her in his heart, and wandering across prairies, a lost and lonely boy once again.

He wouldn't eat; she wasn't hungry.

Bell boarded the waiting wagon and coughed impatiently. A shotgun glinted beside him, protection against the debris of war.

Linda rose and walked gravely to where Canada sat on the veranda steps.

"Canada," she said gently. "When you think of me, slip outside in the night and watch the North Star, and remember me with love. At night, I'll watch it too, and maybe we'll both be looking at it at the same time, some time. You'll always be in my heart, like the North Star."

He glanced up to her with tormented eyes.

She held a hand to him and he took it speechlessly. Then she walked somberly to the wagon and he watched her rattle off, out of the lamplight, and into the eternal night.

CHAPTER SIXTEEN

Canada climbed aboard Crowbait in the gray of first dawn and then led the two Thoroughbreds out of the 30-Mile corrals and up the hushed, pine-walled road into the Bulls. The McFarlands, in despair, had left him in the cushioned rocker on the veranda, rocking sporadically, staring out upon falling stars and lost angels.

He turned into his own ranch road and reined up at his own silent cabin in the rosy light of a clouded sunrise. It was a sorry place, he thought. Small, the handiwork of a small-spirited man who had never dreamed large. Empty and desolate like himself.

He loosed the stallion and mare in a front corral, and then thought better of it and shooed them into a hidden rear one behind the log barn. It wouldn't fool anyone, he supposed. He pitched them some native hay and walked to his little cabin. It was barren and dirty; pilgrims, pack rats, and the sifting winds had turned a living home into a dead shell.

He would clean it up later. He had saddles to gather from the cave, and possibly some of his horses. He had no idea what, if anything, had happened at the VP. For all he knew it could still be in Preacher Jonas's hands, and the vigilante party scattered through the hills, or dead.

He eased up on Crowbait again, thinking to find out. Not that he cared one way or another. A sort of obliviousness had settled upon him. Life might continue, would have to continue because he was no coward, but it would be mechanical, a blotting up of endless time.

He turned off on the VP road, with Crowbait's hooves echoing hollowly through the empty land. He was still managing the VP, he supposed. He would do his duty if he could. He climbed a long grade and passed between twin pillars of sandstone and started down the far side.

"Hold it, mister," a voice snapped. "Hands high."

Canada paused wearily and raised hands slowly, not caring much. He turned to face two cowboys, one a freckle-faced kid; the other a thin dark-haired man with mean blue eyes.

"Got us another hardcase!" the kid chortled.

"I'm Canada Parker. My spread is over north of 30-Mile. I'm a neighbor of the Van Pelts. Also managing the place for them," Canada said slowly.

"Likely story. Bareback, just as you were busting loose like all the rest of those hardcases. Well, we got most of yuh, and now you're one more for the necktie party."

The mean-eyed one said nothing but held a big shotgun steady. The kid's hands whirled, and Canada felt a lariat settle over him. The kid yanked it tight around Canada's torso, pinning his arms.

"Just so you ain't getting any notions, horse thief!"

"You going to hang a man before finding out if he's guilty?" Canada asked slowly.

"Your bein' here is proof enough," the kid joked. "There ain't any virgins in a whorehouse." He laughed at his own simile.

They prodded Canada forward.

"Mebbe we should string him here; that's a fair piece back," the kid said, trying to rile his prisoner.

Canada didn't give a damn.

The kid rode up, loosened the lariat and then tightened it around Canada's neck.

"Now, beg a little," the kid cried, tugging the line.

But Canada didn't give a damn.

The kid yanked hard, pulling Canada off his barebacked gelding. He landed heavily, and his chest hurt.

"Going to let me get back up?" he asked leadenly.

The kid laughed. "Walk," he said.

Canada walked, leading his gelding. He was getting riled up after all. For the first time in hours his thoughts were not upon Linda.

"You strung up some innocents at Roundup," he said acidly.

"No one in Polarski's place was innocent," the mean-eyed older one said, breaking the silence.

"How about the Pinkerton agent who set it up, got names, identified the leaders, told you where to go? How about him? Hanging from a limb!"

There was silence.

"Fat Son Lee was head of the Denver office of Pinkerton's. He made it possible for you to sweep the Bulls clean without much loss. So you hung him," Canada rasped.

"The Celestial? The swamper?" the kid laughed. "You're telling tall tales, hardcase."

"He was a doctor among other things,"

311

Canada raged.

"Now I know you're loco, hardcase!"

They walked into the VP yard, and Canada saw six more bodies dangling. There were ranchers and drovers everywhere; the pens were full of bawling animals, and dust-bitten men were reading brands. Far out on the meadows there were more cowboys driving bunches in from remote valleys.

"Where's Fireball Fenton?" Canada barked. "The 30-Mile foreman?"

"Never heard of him," the kid said.

"He knows me. Find him," Canada snapped.

"Sure he does, hardcase," the kid joked.

They passed through chaos. Canada glanced sadly at the somber ranch house, somehow desecrated by this mob.

"Got another, hey, Turley?" someone yelled happily.

"Who's in charge? I want to see the man in charge," Canada fumed.

"Granville Stuart ain't here, hardcase. We're just havin' our own party."

They passed a pen with 30-Mile cattle in it and Canada spotted Fireball on the far rail, disputing a brand with some drover.

"Fireball!" he roared amid the mayhem. "Goddammit, there he is; let me talk to him."

The kid laughed and yanked the line. Canada hit the dirt. He pulled himself up slowly — his chest hurt again — and then bulled into the freckled youngster. He was weak and tired and likely to get shot, but it didn't matter. He was mad.

He pummeled the kid. He slashed fists into his gut. He kneed the cowboy. But the kid laughed and yanked the rope, sending Canada sprawling again. Then the kid nailed Canada with blows that landed like sledges. His lung hurt. Someone yanked the rope until he choked. They dragged him through dirt, choking, wheezing, gasping. Laughter. Whistles.

A shot.

"Stop it," a man roared.

Fireball Fenton, big, ornery, and swinging a pistol butt that landed viciously on a dozen skulls and shoulders, bulled into the middle and yanked the strangling noose loose.

"I'll shoot the sonofabitch who touches him," Fireball bellowed. "He's the manager of the VP, goddammit!" The big foreman cocked his pistol and aimed at the mean-eyed drover. "I'll stomp you into dirt," he roared.

They backed off. Canada gasped for air.

"Vigilante justice," he wheezed. "Thanks,

Fireball."

He stood up shakily, winded and battered.

"This man is a horse trainer with his own spread here in the Bulls," Fireball thundered. "His horses are branded CP, same as his name. Some were altered to a Bar OB Bar. I seen that myself. Now he's gonna tally VP cattle and he's goin' tuh count horses, including foals and yearlings, just in case you were of a mind to lay a hand on some. You're some bunch, you spitheads, thinkin' to get you all a nice bronc. I got eyes! I seen 'em hid around. Bring 'em in! Every last one!"

Horses appeared. Drovers untied them from odd dark corners everywhere. Some emerged from the barn. Others were led down slopes.

"One thing more," Fireball roared. "Parker has a few CP cows. Any stuff altered from a CP is his."

He dusted off the horse trainer with his hat.

"Come on, Canada, let's go inside and talk," the old foreman growled.

They sat at the kitchen table where they could watch the mayhem in the yard. Canada still shook with pent up rage and fear, but in here Linda flooded through him. Linda's kitchen. Linda's bedroom. Sorrel hair, soft in lamplight. Green eyes, lifted up to his . . .

He had lost his hat somewhere, he realized as he ran a dusty hand through his hair.

"They almost strung you," Fireball said morosely.

"They did hang three innocents in Roundup. Including the Pinkerton agent, the Chinese . . ." Canada said bitterly.

"A Pinkerton man?" Fireball gasped. "There'll be murder warrants then. Or maybe the agency will handle it their own way. They often do."

"The Chinese was a doctor. A scholar in several fields," Canada said.

Fireball sagged. "We split up. Half went into Roundup, half down here to the VP. I took this group 'cause I know this southern Bulls country. If I'd of been with the others I'd of seen a part of it."

He shook his head.

"The doctor saved my life! Got me down to your place before I died," Canada whispered. "He risked everything for us."

They stared moodily at their coffee.

"We're missing that Preacher one. He was probably the leader of this ring. Also his sidekick, the bantam with the beard."

"The bantam's dead," Canada said.

"Kicked in the head and stomped by Crowbait."

"I saw you training that horse with that sawdust injun you rigged. Never did figger it was anything but a dimestore trick," the foreman said.

"Crowbait saved our lives."

"What are yuh going ta do next?"

Canada slumped. "I don't know. Collect my gear from our hideout. Sleep. Go back to my place and work. Keep an eye on these Herefords until I get the word."

Fenton grinned slowly. "Did you know those hardcases slipped Hereford bulls into every cow bunch? Every bloomin' herd in central Montana's going tuh be upgraded."

Canada smiled wanly. He didn't much care.

One by one the ranch crews pulled out, driving their beeves, until only the 30-Mile crew remained. Fireball helped Canada brand the weanling Herefords and pasture them. They buried the hardcases in a separate plot behind the barn, and no one felt very sorry, for it was the 30-Mile that had been wounded most grievously.

Canada's horse herd had grown mysteriously. The drovers had added range broncs to it, he figured. But he was down six beeves.

McFarland's loyal drovers helped Canada

drive the horses to his own spread. The move dovetailed with their own drive of 30-Mile beeves back to McFarland grass. They cut the horses and Canada's cattle at his gate, doffed their hats, and sang their way down the lonesome road.

Canada watched his good horses fan out on the high grass, and then spurred Crowbait and his packhorse up to the empty cabin. It was a moment he had been dreading, and the somber shadows of evening didn't lift his spirits any.

He eased the panniers off the packhorse at the cabin, and corraled the horses.

He was pitching hay to them when Preacher emerged from the shadowed barn.

"Hullo, pilgrim," the gray man said softly. "Lord be praised, I found you . . ."

Canada whirled and threw the pitchfork savagely, impulsively. Two tines pierced Preacher's belly, sliding deep. Preacher staggered back, fell into the haystack with the fork protruding from him.

He grunted in animal pain.

"Gutshot," he rasped. "It's the same as gutshot. Slow bleeding. Fork in manure, too. Godalmighty . . ."

He coughed, and tears rolled up in him.

"Pilgrim, I just repented. Down on my knees. Told the Lord I'd change . . . told him . . . told him . . ."

The man's breath came raggedly and sweat broke out on him.

"I was going to be partners; I like your horses. Partners. Train . . . sell. . . . Respectable living, upright. . . . See? I ain't wearin' a gun. Threw it away . . ."

Canada swallowed hard. He struck the blow impulsively, and now dread filled him. He was one. He, too, was one. He should have taken the man to the law if he could.

"I'll pull it out," he cried wildly, grabbing the fork. The man screamed.

"Don't touch it!" he begged. "Devil's fork. Stabbed by the devil . . . pitchfork . . . Godalmighty it hurts."

Canada stood helplessly while the man raved and sobbed and died. It was an endless half hour, the worst he had known, watching the man's life ebb from internal bleeding.

"God forgive you," Preacher whispered at the end.

Canada gazed somberly as death shadowed into him. The man who had killed so many and had caused still more to die. The man had asked forgiveness for Canada.

Canada wasn't all that sure he needed forgiving. It had been pure self-defense against a dangerous outlaw. He shuddered.

It was dark.

He was always burying people, he thought irritably. He found the old spade and a likely place far down the hill, away from his home. He worked in the cool gloom. The man wasn't so terribly different from lots of folks he knew, he decided as he shoveled. Using God, talking religion to be respectable. Turning the whole thing around until God was just a slave at Preacher's service, and all the virtues were harnessed to his vice. Canada shoveled steadily as the stars appeared, one by one.

Trouble was, Preacher went further than other folks. The worse he got the more saintly he tried to be in his own eyes. He had to keep his lie and shut out the terrible glimpses of his true self that pressed upon him from time to time.

It was black. Canada couldn't get the hole very deep. Rock everywhere. This Preacher, he knew the hardcases. They wanted to like themselves, too. He used it, Preacher did. Talking the Good Book at them, making thieves and gunslingers somehow feel more respectable.

He sighed and walked up the hill to the haystack. The pitchfork — the devil's pitchfork, he thought grimly — came out hard. He drove it deep into the clean earth. He lifted the man. There was no weight to him. He had all will, all evil will, and no flesh. Canada carried him down to the hole and covered him over in the starlight, tired.

Some force stayed him when he gathered the shovel and pick to leave. A breeze made the pines whisper in the glassy black.

"Lord God," he said into the cold night. "Seems I'm always doing this. I won't judge this man. That's for you. He trampled on all your laws, every one, I imagine, and yet he was cryin' up to you the whole time. Wantin' not to. So's I felt dirty every time he said your name in that voice. I'm just sayin' how I felt, not judgin'. Anyway, he's yours now. Judge him kindly if you would. I'd like to be judged kindly myself — that was my pitchfork, Lord."

He walked alone up the slope to the cabin, hulking small and lonely in the dark. He swept it out. The rest he would do later. He stuffed some fresh hay into his tick and fell asleep, remembering Linda lying on that very tick one March morning.

He didn't have the pain he felt when Linda left, nor even the dread of loneliness he once had. But he knew, nonetheless, that he was lower than he'd ever been. Sleep was all he wanted. The days he'd just as soon forget.

He settled into his old training routines, but his strength was half gone. He needed a nap two or three times a day. He realized his smashed chest would never get any better, and he began to resign himself to it.

Something was forever gone from his life. The thing now was to endure, keep on struggling, rebuild, forget. But the latter he couldn't do. Always, the image of Linda was before him. He saved up thoughts to tell her — but she wasn't there to talk to. When he wanted to hug her, there was nothing to hug. Only the North Star, white in the night.

Sometimes he threw his arms around the neck of a horse, liking the clean, slightly acrid smell of the animal and the pleasure of holding something warm and alive. It was not something he wanted anyone to see, this hugging.

The vision never really left him. The green eyes, the swirling sorrel hair. It was nothing he could help. The manhood in him urged him to set the vision aside, redouble his efforts, turn to new life. He did. He rose earlier, drilled the grudging horses until he dropped with exhaustion. And still the vision of Linda haunted him.

A pleasant letter from Mr. Bell arrived, with a check for services rendered the VP ranch. It would soon be sold; the stock auctioned. The NP would handle it all, henceforth. So the last tie to Linda was gently severed.

The frosts came. Canada rarely left his horse ranch. Sales dropped, but those few who bought were unusually pleased. He took to riding the Thoroughbreds on the frosty fall days. There was a flat hay meadow where he could let them run, and he enjoyed the breathtaking speed of them during the gallops. In the spring he would begin breeding, and his mind turned often to possible combinations, especially among his quarter mares.

Fireball dropped by from time to time, obviously on a scouting mission from the McFarlands. It was painful. They talked spasmodically over some java, but Canada, lost in reverie, never mentioned the summer or inquired after his old friends and neighbors.

"Dammit, Canada," he grumbled, "you can't just pull the lid of the coffin over you."

"I'm not. I work hard every day. I'm enduring. I've lost my strength but I'm doing more now than ever. These horses are the best I've ever trained," said Canada calmly.

"That ain't what I mean," Fireball flared. "You know damn well what I'm talkin' about. You're a danged hermit. You can't let any woman do that to you."

"No woman did anything to me," Canada smiled. "It's my choice."

Fireball stared doubtfully at him.

"Well then it's a bum choice. You're just pityin' yourself."

"No, I don't think so. I've come to like the solitude."

That's as far as it went. It was a half-truth, Canada knew.

The cold made his chest ache. He spent less time with his horses and more cutting wood. It was slow going now. Three pieces and rest, three and rest.

Not long before Christmas, Anne came in a buckboard.

"Damn you, Canada, why don't you come see us?"

He smiled, helped her out of the wagon. She wore a heavy sheepskin coat and woolly chaps, like the winter gear of the men on her spread.

It was good to see her after all, this brown-haired, tan, dark-eyed curvaceous woman.

"I'm gonna get right down to business," she announced, settling beside the stove. "And you're gonna listen, you pinhead."

Canada braced himself for The Lecture. He'd heard it from Fireball often enough.

But she surprised him.

"Linda Van Pelt was the most special person you've ever known, wasn't she?" Anne said softly.

Her question was melting. She didn't wait for him to respond. "I saw her and I agree. I'm glad you loved her, Canada. You picked a rare one, a girl to ride the river with. Usually the beautiful ones have airs. But she didn't. She was all honesty and loyalty and sweetness and common sense. Don't know how she had so much good sense, being so rich like that. And not just pretty, but *beautiful.* And radiant. With those green eyes and her New Yorky way of talkin'. Be glad you loved her, Canada. The world's most fortunate and powerful men could do no better than to win her love."

Anne talked softly, urgently, reaching something in Canada, joy and torment alike.

"She had a sweetness, oh, I see things, Canada Parker. It was real, and so was the wisdom she had. And the loyalty for you. They say James Reed was a man among men, and she sure was his daughter . . ."

Canada nodded numbly.

"Canada, she's gone. She's not coming back. You've got to let go."

"I've tried."

"I know you have, you old hermit. But

you can't let go in a vacuum. As long as you're alone up here, you couldn't cut loose even if you tried. Don't you see?"

"That's true," he said sadly. He rather liked the way the talk was going. She was saying things . . . talking in ways he never saw before in Anne McFarland.

"I came to bushwack you for Christmas, but that's just a damned excuse," she said solemnly. "I've gotta grit my teeth and say some forward things."

"Huh?"

"I've got — some burdens of my own. I'm heading for thirty and no one's put a brand on me. I'm tired of puttering around the house, looking after Dad. I want to get married, Canada."

"Are you proposing?" he grinned.

"Yes I am, dammit! I've waited long enough for you to. You're the only one for me, all I've ever wanted."

Canada was suddenly aware that Anne had her own prettiness, soft and desirable and friendly.

"But I tell you, Canada, I can't wait any more. I go to those box-lunch socials and sometimes some of those fellas lay a hand to me — I know I've got a few handfuls," she grinned. "And I slap those hands off because I'm supposed to, and because I've always wanted you. Well, I'm getting tired of it. Next one puts a hand on me, I'll likely put his other hand on me, too. I'm going plumb crazy, damn you, Canada!"

He laughed suddenly, laughed happily.

"Look," she said urgently. "I can't replace Linda inside of you. No other woman ever could. But I can give you all I've got. Maybe not all she's got, but all of me. I love you, Canada, damn you. I love you. Oh, sonofabitch, now I've gone and done it!" she blushed.

Her composure was gone, and Canada saw wetness in her eyes. And he saw love. Not only in her, but in himself. Somehow, it was new to him, but it was there. He lifted her from her chair, and gently hugged her.

"Canada? Canada? I love you."

The little cabin was quiet on a snowy afternoon.

"How about a Christmas weddin'?" he said tenderly. "We'll get busy and raise us some brown-haired rascally boys and some girls with your dimples. Maybe three or five or a dozen."

"Damn you to hell, Canada Parker, makin' me sit around all fall," she blustered. "You come down to 30-Mile right now."

"After a while," he grinned, kissing her.